DUBLIN WHERE THE PALM TREES GROW

Dublin Where the Palm Trees Grow

HUGO HAMILTON

faber and faber
LONDON · BOSTON

First published in Great Britain in 1996
by Faber and Faber Limited
3 Queen Square London WC1N 3AU

Phototypeset by Avon Dataset Ltd, Warwickshire
Printed in England by Mackays of Chatham plc, Chatham, Kent

A CIP record for this book
is available from the British Library
ISBN 0–571–17693–3

The author would like to express his thanks to Dermot Bolger, whose idea it
was initially to put together this collection; to David Marcus and Tony
Glavin of *The Irish Press* (New Irish Writing) and Caroline Walsh of *The Irish
Times* for publishing many of these stories; to Bernard and Mary Loughlin at
the Tyrone Guthrie Centre at Annamakerrig, where some of the stories were
written; and to John Fairleigh for his support.

2 4 6 8 10 9 7 5 3 1

For Birch and Jimmy

Contents

The Supremacy of Grief

One eye is half shut while the other is open. So we don't know whether it's drunkenness or whether he is looking out with deep anger. He hasn't said a word for a while. His arms and legs are limp, restrained by the shape of the armchair. We don't know whether he is about to fall asleep or whether he will soon begin to mutter or talk, or even shout. Whether he might say something terribly funny or terribly tragic or whether he is building up a general resentment of all around him. One eye is ajar, but the other is fully open looking across the room at the opposite wall. Anyone looking at his eyes might draw upon himself the full force that lies behind them.

He's had a lot to drink of course. Not without reason. His wife Sarah died only five days ago. Even at the funeral, he was unpredictable, showing little sign of emotion and listening to the many semi-sincere condolences either with too much interest or an obvious lack of it. He looked at people's shoes. At the graveside, he nudged his brother to point out the extraordinary hat which one of Sarah's relatives wore. 'Would you ever look at that hat, for Christ sake,' he said almost for everyone to hear. And later in the day, there was the row with the same brother for turning his wife's funeral into a party. 'It's just an excuse for a party. Have you forgotten that my wife has just died?' The outburst was enough to return a degree of solemnity to the gathering and to remind everyone that nobody had more right than he to find solace in laughter. That all mirth was at his discretion.

The next day it was decided that he should spend a few days in Dublin. Nobody knows when the real grief sets in. Nobody knows what a man alone in his grief might do. They had no children and it was considered better or safer for him to be in company for a while longer.

At his own instructions, his two sisters Grainne and Marita had gone through Sarah's possessions sharing what clothes and jewellery they could use and arranging for the rest to be disposed of so that no trace of his wife except the wedding photo and the well-kept gardens would remain on his return. Then he was brought to Dublin in the car, stopping frequently for drinks to hold back the emptiness. Arriving well after seven in the evening, he began to embrace and kiss everyone excessively saying, 'What a feckin' life?' 'What a shagging life, eh?'; to which nobody knew how to respond, not knowing whether he was serious or not, other than to hand him a further gin and tonic and direct him to the armchair where he has been sitting ever since. The drink is on a small table beside him, virtually untouched.

His two sisters sit on the sofa together discussing the details of the funeral with their cousin Deirdre. They throw occasional glances over at Damien in the armchair. Grainne or Auntie Grainne has just shifted her position in order to cross her legs and feeling the renewed comfort in her muscles, continues to describe the funeral. 'It was magnificent.' To emphasize, she shakes her head very slowly while looking earnestly into the listener's eyes.

The two children in the house keep running from the kitchen into the sitting-room and back. At one point, they stop to look at Uncle Damien's watch. Without altering the one-and-a-half ratio in his eyes, he smiles at them and urges them to try the watch on themselves. One of them walks around proudly with the large watch while the other clamours to have a go. They are wearing their best dresses with ribbons at the back. Their father, Paul, who sits on the other side of the fireplace, tells them to give the watch back before they break it. In doing this, they giggle because Uncle Damien makes it difficult by spreading his fingers out. The girls look intensely at the tufts of hair on his fingers and along the side of his hand. They look at his buttons, his face and his ears. They soon disappear again into the kitchen where their mother is cooking.

Uncle Damien looks at a large drink stain below Paul's chair without seeing it. He stares at the two objects on the mantelpiece without absorbing them. The miniature wooden snake emerging from a basket and the brass tortoise which can be used as an ashtray.

Auntie Grainne has just glanced at Uncle Damien and turns to Paul.

'Paul, you haven't told Damien about your new job.' Turning to Damien, she repeats the catalyst. 'Did you know that Paul had a fantastic new job with IBM?'

'Yah bugger!' Uncle Damien looks over at Paul. 'Well, congratulations. I always knew you were marked out for it.'

Paul is like most people. He talks about his job. He prefers to talk about anything but Uncle Damien's wife. He doesn't want to stir the heavy sediment of grief. His conversation ignores the most prominent issue on Uncle Damien's mind. The two sisters on the couch have also been avoiding any mention of Sarah. They don't talk about her face. They don't talk about her things. They won't quote her. They won't mention her absence or her former presence. It is almost as if Sarah had been a very bad woman.

Every time the children open the door of the sitting-room, a faint smell of soup comes in with them from the kitchen. The smell is foreign.

Uncle Damien's mouth is sealed. It looks as though he is about to make a very serious observation. It also looks as though he is about to say something very funny. When the children interrupt to look at his watch again, he continues to look at Paul without listening. He waits for a moment and turns to the girls.

'I want you to do something for me. Will you go in to your mummy and tell her that if it's not duck à l'orange, I'm not eating it. Duck à l'orange, have you got that?'

Uncle Damien looks at them seriously. His speech is slow and deliberate. The children repeat 'Duck à l'orange' and run away into the kitchen from where the vague smell of food is impossible to identify.

The two sisters, Auntie Grainne and Auntie Marita are both angled slightly towards Deirdre who is telling them about a recent burglary at her house. Above the mantelpiece hangs a painted picture of a boat leaning to one side on a strand, the tide having receded far away into the distance. Behind Uncle Damien there are green plants, bushy ferns and drooping stalks; enough for him to hide in thick undergrowth if he were to move back. The curtains are a mass of falling leaves.

Uncle Damien moves forward to speak to Paul, much in the same way as he might talk about something he read in the paper.

'Do you know that I had a very, very beautiful wife called Sarah?'

Paul is surprised at the words. Uncle Damien is looking at him and the pause demands a response. Paul searches and rejects all the possible answers. 'She was indeed!' or 'She must have been!' or 'No doubt about it!' After a moment, when it's almost too late, Paul says: 'I think every-body knows that.'

'Do you think so really?' Uncle Damien preserves the equilibrium between a joke and something very serious on his face. It seems as though he doesn't need to blink.

In an effort to punctuate the conversation, Paul adds 'Definitely.' But Uncle Damien continues.

'There's only one serious regret that I have.' He pauses again.

'There's something I should have told her. I always wanted to tell her, even as far back as ten years ago. I kept meaning to tell her about it but I always stopped myself when the moment came. I thought I would save her the trouble.

'Do you know that even on her deathbed, I had a great urge to tell her everything but I just couldn't. And now it's too late. It's the one thing that kills me.'

Paul wants to ask him what it was but won't let himself. He doesn't want to appear inquisitive. He expects Uncle Damien to tell him anyway. But the children rush in the door saying, 'She said you're very, very bold. You have to come in for your dinner now.'

'Is it duck à l'orange? If it isn't, I'm not eating.'

'Come in for your dinner,' they shout.

'I can't! I'm stuck in this chair. You're going to have to pull me out.'

His left eye remains half shut. His arms are still limp along the armrests. The girls make an effort to pull them but they only make him look heavier and sleepier.

'Look, girls, stop friggin' about. One of you pull this arm and you pull the other.'

Paul stands up and waits by the door, smiling at the effort his daughters need to extract Uncle Damien from the chair. With a little more success, they manage to pull him forward.

They believe that their own strength has achieved this and pull even harder.

'Come on, girls, you'll have to do better than that,' Uncle Damien says. They pull again and he moves forward a little more. But instead of standing up, he begins to sink deliberately and heavily to his knees and when they keep pulling, he finally collapses on to his back on the floor. The older of the girls says, 'Oh no,' and giggles.

They try to pull him up again but Uncle Damien is playing dead. One eye is still half open but the other is still completely shut now. Paul discovers by looking at his head why Uncle Damien always carries a half-funny, half-serious expression. It's the shape of the head. It's still a schoolboy's head.

Dara has come in from the kitchen to tell everyone to sit down for dinner. When she finds Uncle Damien on the floor, she laughs and says, 'Uncle Damien, come on now, time for dinner.' One of the children lets go of an arm which falls loosely to the floor.

Aunt Marita gets up from the sofa followed by the others. Deirdre walks straight out to go to the bathroom. Aunt Marita begins to talk to Damien like a child.

'Damien, what are you doing on the floor? Up you get now, dinner's ready.'

But Uncle Damien seems to ignore everyone and continues to play dead. Nobody believes him. Everybody is sure he's only putting it on. Even though he looks completely lifeless, they know he's alive. Dead people generally look like they're grinning underneath. Aunt Marita doesn't like it. It's beneath his dignity to act dead like that. She reaches down and begins to pull at his arm.

'Come on, Damien, up you get now. You're keeping everybody waiting.'

Dara joins in and begins to pull at the other arm saying,

'The food is going cold.' But Uncle Damien even ignores this plea for courtesy and remains lifeless with his dead man's grin. Aunt Marita almost stumbles with the effort. 'Damien, you're too heavy,' she says. They manage to pull his shoulders up but his head falls back and his Adam's apple is pointing at the ceiling.

Nobody knows the difference between a dead man and a man who wants to play dead. They look the same. Perhaps they also feel the same. Nobody knows the difference between a dead man and a man whose wife is dead and who himself is acting dead.

The two women pull energetically. They have given up pleading with Uncle Damien and have begun to plead with Paul to help them. Paul declines and remains at the door with one hand in his pocket. He doesn't want to help a man who doesn't want help. If he were to join in, it would make Uncle Damien look helpless.

Auntie Marita is breathless. Everybody is now concerned with getting Uncle Damien up. His half-closed eye still stares up at nothing. The more they pull the heavier he seems to get. They have stopped depending on Uncle Damien's own strength and demand help from Paul. Dara looks up at Paul seriously.

'Paul, come on now. All the food is going cold. Give us a hand.'

Paul capitulates under this renewed pressure and goes over to join in. But as he takes hold of Uncle Damien's wrist and begins to pull slowly, the eyes open wide and look straight up at Paul. We don't know whether the eyes are opened in anger or in disbelief. Whether he opened them to see something or say something. To perceive or transmit. Whether they are open to find out if he's alive or whether to tell Paul that there was never any doubt about it. Paul immediately releases his hold on the wrist and steps back.

Uncle Damien gets up of his own accord.

As they walk in to take their places at the table, the thought of food makes them forget. Nobody remembers what Uncle Damien looks like dead.

Nazi Christmas

It began with the man in the fish shop saying 'Achtung!' and all the customers turning around to look at us. Even the people outside under the row of naked turkeys and hanging pheasants stared in through the window. We were exposed. Germans. War criminals using Ireland as a sanctuary. There was a chance they might have overlooked the whole thing if it wasn't for the man in the fish shop trying out some more of his German. All the stuff he had picked up from films like *Von Ryan's Express* and *The Great Escape*.

'Guten Morgen,' he said leaning over the counter, then leaning back with an explosive laugh that acted as a trademark for his shop. Our mother was shy of these friendly, red-faced Irishmen. She smiled at all the people in the shop and they smiled back silently. That was the thing about Ireland. They were all so friendly.

'We haff ways of making you talk,' he said to us whenever we refused to perform for the benefit of his customers and say a few words of German. Like our mother, we were too shy and unable to respond to these contortions of language.

'Halt! We must not forgetten der change.' There was something about us that made people laugh, or whisper, or stop along the street quite openly to ask the most bizarre questions; something that stuck to us like an electronic tag.

It was as though the man in the fish shop had let out this

profane secret about us. The word was out. Our assumed identity as Irish children was blown. Everywhere we went, the German past floated on the breeze after us. 'Heil Hitler!' we heard them shout, on the way to Mass, on the way to school, on the way back from the shops. Our mother told us to ignore them. We were not Nazis.

When we were on our own they jumped out behind us or in front of us howling their warcries. It was all 'Donner und Blitzen', and 'Achtung! Get the Krauts'. We lacked the Irish instinct for blending in with the crowd, that natural expertise of human camouflage. It didn't help that Eichmann went on trial for war crimes when I was around five years old. So I was called Eichmann, or sometimes Göring. My older brother usually went under Hitler or Himmler, and the greeting 'Sieg Heil!' was generally accompanied by a neat karate chop on the back of the neck.

It didn't help either that on those shopping trips into town before Christmas, our mother talked to us in German on the bus. Just when we began to enjoy the comfort of anonymity, she would say 'Lass das sein' ('Stop that') in a harsh German tone and the passengers would turn around to stare again. But once we saw the lights in the city and the vast toy departments it was easy to forget. On the way home she told stories and sang Christmas songs like 'O Tannenbaum' with the shopping bags stacked on the seats beside us and the winter sky lighting up pink beyond the roofs of the houses. It was a sign that the angels were baking. And at home there was always the smell of baking.

When we got home there were sweets laid out in the hallway, on the stairs, sometimes across our pillows at night, and when we asked how they got there she said: 'the angels'. She made 'marzipan potatoes', small marzipan marbles coated with cinnamon. On the morning of the sixth of December we came down to find a plate for each of us filled with sweets and a glazed 'Männeken' – a little man with raisin eyes that lasted for ever. The St Nicholas plates stood on the *Truhe* in the hall, a large oak trunk made in 1788 to store vestments. It was part of her heirloom from Kempen. Everything inside our house was German.

Everything outside was Irish, or imported from Britain. The other houses all had coloured fairy-lights on Christmas trees in the windows. We envied those coloured lights. At the same time we knew we were the only house with real candles, almost like a sign to the outside, a provocation. Most of our clothes and our toys came in parcels from German relatives.

The snow seemed to be a German invention too. Thick flakes fell in Ireland that Christmas and made our mother think of home. There was never any snow again at Christmas; perhaps afterwards in January but never on Christmas Day itself. Somehow Ireland had committed itself more towards the milder Mediterranean climate. With the undercurrent of the Gulf Stream, people here had grown a variety of palm tree that leaned towards the tropical; palm trees that formed the centrepiece of front gardens and patios. Guest houses along the coast expanded the sub-tropical illusion by hanging nameplates like Santa Maria or Stella Maris from their palms.

Snow was another import which remained mostly in the imagination, on Christmas cards, on top of Christmas cakes, in the form of cotton wool on the roof of the crib. But that year the snow was real; full white snow that took away the seaside appearance and transformed the streets into a fairy-tale of winter. It was our Christmas. Our father put on his favourite Christmas record of the Cologne Children's Choir and the house was filled with the bells of Cologne Cathedral ringing out across the sea to Dublin. There was the taste of German food, pretzels and *Lebkuchen* and exotic gifts from Germany.

We might as well have been in Kempen where our mother came from, kneeling in front of the crib as we prayed and sang in German with the white candles reflected in my father's glasses and the smell of pine merging with the smell of *Glühwein* in the front room.

Later, we went out to build a snowman in the front garden and it was only when we entered a snowball fight with other children in the street that we realized we were back in Ireland; where children had scooped snow from the low walls or where the cars had skidded and exposed the raw street underneath. We went from one garden to the next looking for new untouched sheets of snow, where the street was still under a dream. And when all the other children disappeared inside for Christmas dinner, we decided to go to the football field to see how deep the snow was there.

It seemed like a good idea until we were ambushed in the lane by a gang of boys we had never seen before. Amelia and I ran away into the field through the opening in the barbed-wire fence, but they had caught Karl and pushed him against the wall. One of them held a stick across his neck. 'You Nazi bastard,' they said.

Amelia and I shouted to let him go. She threatened to tell on them but it was a frail plea. We were trapped.

'Get them,' one of them said and three or four of the boys ran into the field after us. There was no point in screaming for help either because nobody would hear.

'You Nazi bastard,' they said again to Karl. Then they twisted his arm up behind his back and made him walk towards the field where Amelia and I had already been caught behind a line of eucalyptus trees. One of them was forcing snow up Amelia's jumper and she was whining with the effort to fight him off.

Karl said nothing. He had already put into action his plan of inner defiance and was determined to give them nothing but silence, as though they didn't exist, as though they would soon get tired and go away. Amelia stopped resisting and they stopped putting snow under her jacket because she wasn't contributing to the fun. We were told to line up with our backs against the wall of the football field.

The leader of the gang had no fear of the cold. While the other boys blew into their cupped red hands for warmth, he calmly picked up more snow and caked it into a flat icy disc in his palms. We kept repeating in our heads the maxims our mother had taught us: 'The winner yields. Ignore them.' I tried to look as though standing against the wall was exactly what I wanted to be doing at that very moment.

'What will we do with these Nazi fuckers?' the leader asked, holding his stony white disc up to our faces. 'Put them on trial,' somebody said.

They formed a circle around us and discussed how they would proceed with this. There was no point in thinking of escape. One of the boys was pushing a discoloured piece of brown snow towards Karl with the tip of his shoe, whispering to him: 'I'm going to make you eat that.' Amelia started crying again but Karl told her to be quiet.

'OK, Nazi,' the leader said. 'What have you got to say for yourselves?'

'Don't indulge them,' Karl said to us. 'Don't indulge them,' they all mocked and for some of them it was the sign to start speaking in a gibberish of German. 'Gotten, blitzen . . . Himmel.' Another boy started dancing around, trampling a circle in the snow with 'Sieg Heils' until Amelia could no longer contain a short, nervous smile. For the leader it was a sign to hurl his snowball. It hit me in the eye with a flash of white; a hard lump of icy stone that immediately made me hold my face. I was close to tears but I didn't want to let Karl down and give them the satisfaction.

'The Nazi Brothers,' he then announced. 'Guilty or not guilty?'

'Guilty,' they all shouted and they laughed and collected more snow. The trees were being pushed by the wind. Above the white landscape of the football field the sky was darkening and it looked as though it would snow again. Low on the grey sky there were flashes of white or silver seagulls.

'We have to go home now,' Amelia said with a sudden burst of self-righteousness as she moved forward to go. But she was held back. 'You're going nowhere, you SS whore.'

All of it meant little to us. It was as though the terms were being invented there and then, as though they came from somebody's perverse imagination. One of them said something about concentration camps, and gas chambers. Whenever I asked my mother about the Nazis I saw a look in her eyes somewhere between confusion and regret.

'Execute them,' they all shouted. They were looking for signs that one of us might break. The only hope for us was that they might get bored with it all. That they too might be numb with the cold.

The sentence became obvious as they quietly began an industry of snowball-making. Somebody mentioned the 'firing squad'. Some of them laughed and Amelia once more began to cry. They crouched down and collected mounds of snowballs, enough to start another war. Somebody reminded everyone to pack them hard. One of them included the discoloured piece of snow in his armoury and when they all had heaps of white cannonballs ready beside their feet, we waited for the order and watched the leader of the gang mutely raise his hand.

It seemed like an endless wait in which it was possible to think of all kinds of random, irrelevant things like Christmas cake, and marzipan potatoes and the peculiar skull-shaped design of the plum pudding as well as other even more irrelevant things like the three little dials of the gas meter under the stairs, until the hand eventually came down and the piercing shout brought with it a hail of blinding white fire. Karl put his hands up to his eyes. 'It's only snow.'

Above and Beyond

I wasn't able to talk that day. But I had my fists sunk deep into my coat. It's always that way. Whenever I see people, I can say nothing. And the street was fast and full of people. And she was beside me. So I couldn't find anything to say. But it was a good day for us. We were in the city and she had money. And she was as slow as I was. It was cold. Her knuckles were crushed and red and half hidden by the sleeves of her coat. Even though I said nothing, she looked at me again. I don't know if I was smiling because we looked down and saw money falling in the street. All coins rolling away in semicircles. I know the sound of coins very well. And I saw her crushed hands coming up from her pockets. I thought it was water but it was money, more money. I looked at her eyes and I couldn't say anything and I couldn't stop her throwing money down, so I walked away. But she followed me and I stopped. I couldn't hit her so she walked into the shop where I saw her pushing one of the people and spilling more money on the floor. Then she followed me again and tried to kick me because her knuckles were crushed and her face was red. But she couldn't get me because she fell down in the street and I couldn't kick her because it was too late and a Guard had picked her up by the collar. So she started screaming and trying to hit me again and the people stopped to look, so there was nothing I could say. And she tried to hit the Guard and kept on screaming because she has a voice. I don't. I only say what I hear. When I hear somebody say something, I think I've said it myself. And I heard somebody say the Guard was going to take her away.

A crowd has gathered at the end of Talbot Street. They have no time to stop but the sight of people gathered looking in one direction compels them to look. Nothing better to do than to see what others are looking at. A Guard with black leather gloves is holding a girl, a traveller girl, by the collar. He is tall, which makes it look as though her feet don't touch the ground. Her movements lack balance or skill, like an infant. Her whine for liberty is half directed at the crowd, staging pain and brutality. Perhaps their spectator stares might force him to set her free. Her partner stands by, silent, watching her scream.

'Lemme go – lemme go.'

There is something in her hand which she pushes up towards the Guard.

'Have a sniff a that. Go on, why don't ye? Have a sniff.'

Her voice is hoarse like a cat under a caravan. Her teeth sound numb with saliva. She coughs her damp lungs to make him let her go. But he tells her to keep quiet, looking down at her like a flight of concrete steps. The people of Dublin speak like rain.

She's very young. She could be only sixteen. What did she do? She musta done something. Look at her, she can't stand. Your man is no better. I seen her in the shop over there. I seen her pushing a lady. He's got an awful lot of patience with her. I woulda given her a box. I say I'd give her a box in the ear.

She's only young. Would you look at your man? He's footless. It's a rough life, poor thing. She's only about sixteen. Ah, she has it coming.

The Guard's collar is tight with authority. His hand is inside a black glove. His head is under a hat. The street is underfoot. Music comes out from the shops. Bargains face out on the street. The man's eyes are facing out. Onlookers face in towards the girl in the grip of a Guard. A crowd of people knows something. They know she's very young. They know where the bargains are. They know what it's like to put on a new coat. What it's like to put on the old one again. What it's like to be inside a coat. Inside shoes. Under a hat. In the street. On your own. In a crowd. In front of food. Outside music. Under illusion. Inside the law. In front of TVs. Behind husbands. Beside girlfriends. Beyond help. Overlooked. Underestimated. Well informed. Left of centre. Ill-defined. Self-contained. Unattached. Round-shouldered. Sympathetic.

Some of them speak with pity. Some of them know better.

'Ah, they're just awful, them two. I seen her in the shop over there.'

They look at the Guard whose breath touches the girl's head. She tries again to get away. She reminds everyone of the cold. She reminds everyone of their own homes.

A crowd forms of the longing to remain separate. People speak to each other to keep their distance. They gather and divide into a crowd of individuals. They collate and stand looking so as not to be looked at. So as not to be recognized. Fame is the most excessive form of anonymity. And success is pure failure. They watch somebody being arrested for a sense of dignity. People keep budgies to remind themselves of freedom. People keep children so they can forget about themselves. A man joins the crowd so nobody will know he's just got a haircut. A woman in the crowd speaks her mind to let everyone know she's part of the crowd. Another woman adjusts her underwear so that nobody will notice her. Women wear lipstick so people can't see them. You need a crowd so you can look for yourself. You need music so you can hear yourself. You wear shoes so you can stand up. You get on a bus so you can look out. You eat to prove you're alive. You speak to find out what you're on about. You tell people about yourself because you want to know about them. You admit your mistakes so you can go on making mistakes in greater comfort. People stand in the street so that seagulls can fly overhead. You kick a dog so you can feel your foot. You stroke a dog so you can feel your foot another time. You walk the dog because you're afraid of yourself. You eat a sandwich to find out if you're hungry. Pubs are there to keep people away from each other. Shops are there for people to walk past each other. The owner of a shop belongs to his customers. The owner of a car belongs to his car. The man who beats his wife is at her mercy.

While the river stands still, the city moves on. While some let go, others hold on. While a Guard holds out his arm for the crowd, a girl dances beneath his breath. While a woman looks in her bag, a man beside her looks away. While a girl dances, a woman asks her husband for money. You watch the girl while you stand in a crowd. You read a book to confirm that you're not the only one. While you read a book, a couple make love. While people kiss, the city stands still. While Matt Talbot kneels down, a woman gets up to put on her sock. While you turn your back on the girl, it takes place right in front of your eyes. While more people talk, less is being said. While agreements are signed, the sheets are being stained. Ireland unstained shall never be at peace. While somebody looks up, somebody else flinches in sunlight. While somebody remembers his ancestors, a woman's nostrils expand with the smell. While you might be lucky to be alive, you might be unlucky enough to be a republican. While some are afflicted with a good education, some are better off joining the Guards. People stand in the street because they feel more at home. The woman whose home is decorated with hundreds of ornaments, brass ornaments, clocks, commemoration plaques, coats of arms, a bull brought back from Spain, a porcelain grotto from Lourdes, a picture of John F. Kennedy and Pope John, a copper sailing-boat and a silver-plated shoe, can easily get lost among the crowd. The woman who owns a porcelain grotto will see porcelain grottoes all over Dublin. A woman with red shoes will see other women with red shoes. While you might want to be like your friends, everything you own will betray you. Clothes are worn so you can tell people apart. Pubs are there to keep friends apart. You hit somebody so you can get to know them better. You get on better with those you dislike. A cavalry of traffic awaits the instruction to charge while a woman lifts her foot from the pavement. Thomas Moore is on the point of speaking while somebody shoves a tenner in his back pocket. While a woman looks down at her shoes, people keep looking up to politicians. A man with his hand in his pocket disappears into government buildings while pupils with ink on their hands emerge from school with pop idols inscribed on their schoolbags. A hand makes gradual progress underneath a schoolgirl's jumper in the lane by Granby's, while onions are being sliced in Chinese restaurants. People think of the approaching evening as others remember the morning falling away. As a girl shouts under the grip of a Guard, people gather to hide their own feelings. A man stands mute and inert, watching his girl in the grip of a Guard. A blue car arrives with blue flashing light, while somewhere else a man sits down, places his elbows on the table and prepares to take the first bite from a hamburger held up at eye level. A woman in the crowd says, 'But she's so young.' Another woman says, 'They're taking her away.'

The man is unable to say a word because someone in the crowd has already said it. What he wants to say is being said by the crowd. Slowly, he points to the girl's head and on realizing this, she pulls back her hair to uncover an old gash in her skull. The people in the crowd instantly whisper and forget their own pain. While two more Guards step from the blue car, the first Guard breathes on the girl and a woman in the crowd says, 'I don't know.' While nobody knows why she's being taken away, somebody says, 'She must have done something.' While her friend can say nothing, somebody says, 'They're taking her in the car.' And while the man cannot stop her going, somebody says, 'Where are they taking her?' As she resists, holding on to the door of the blue car, somebody says, 'Look, she's not going.' And as the man watches her resisting, the people of Dublin speak like rain. Then she turns to the crowd and shouts, 'What are ye all looking at?' and repeats with screaming dignity, 'What are ye looking at, ye?' and the people in the crowd suddenly begin to move without actually going any-where. And they continue to move as the girl shouts back at them again, 'Go on, look at ye.' As another Guard helps to force her into the car, she turns to him and says, 'Take a sniff a that.' And while the crowd begins to laugh, the Guards become impatient. A fist strikes her in the ribs as her partner stands motionless in the street, now almost becoming part of the crowd watching her while somebody says, 'Ah, there's no need for that.' And others quietly repeat, 'There's no need for that. She's far too young.' Now he sees her through the windows sitting in the back seat of the blue car. She's being taken away for the sake of the crowd. She sits in the back seat to remind everyone that they're standing in the street. Then she begins to beat her fists down on the necks of the two Guards sitting in the front seats and the crowd begins to laugh again while the man stands mute and the crowd says, 'Look she's hittin' the two in front. Would you look at her.' Now the crowd almost becomes proud of her. She's one of their own. And the first Guard gets into the back seat beside her and places the fist within its black glove in her ribs, while somebody says, 'There's no need for that'. And the blue car pulls away while her partner is left behind. As the people disperse, he remains in that spot. While the people stop talking, he stops saying anything, and his fists are sunk deep in his coat.

The Irish Worker

The rattling stopped. The wind gathered again to renew its attack on the window. It seemed to gather in the trees and over the houses and possibly around the spire of St Paul's Church. It gathered and sometimes ignored my window completely only to come back with surprise and stronger gusts. The window rattled again, knocked back and forth in its wooden frame. It had no pattern. Sometimes the wind had so much force that it held the window firm under its pressure. Then you could hear the whistle and wheezing more clearly. It was an urgent sound. Only when the gust slackened its resolve again did the window renew its irregular, random banging.

My earliest theory about storms as a boy was that they were caused by giants blowing at each other. That's when I was four. Occasionally, my mother gets out the old school essay to show it to me. Big, freestanding letters from the alphabet. She says I haven't written anything like it since. I haven't replaced the theory either. All I can think of is the constant rattling. It keeps me awake.

I would love to know everything there is to know about wind motion. Set up detailed charts and observations about squalls, gusts, gales and even the smallest buffeting. I'd love to know things that could never be contradicted. Perhaps you could study the wind by colouring it, the same as you could observe a pink liquid curling around in a glass of water or milk clouding in tea. You get an idea how wind moves by watching my father burning leaves and weeds in the garden. It catches the smoke and sends it creeping along the garden wall and then suddenly up straight over the wall where it disperses quickly. Other times, you could watch the smoke seeping up for ages through the moist leaves and drifting down the garden from you and then the wind suddenly blows back and the thick smoke stings your eyes. If it didn't dissipate so quickly, smoke would tell you a lot about wind really. Clouds are too bulky.

The relentless gusts rattling the window tell me nothing. They're too erratic. Finally they propel me out of the bed and over to my desk. I tear up a foolscap page and fold it over and over until it becomes the size of a fat stamp. I tear up another sheet and do the same. I stand there in the bottoms of my pyjamas with the light on. Instead of theory I have practical answers. The thick, folded foolscap pages fit neatly between the frame and the window. Under the blankets again, I listen to the hush.

Outside, new chestfuls and cheekfuls of gathered wind blow against the window. But the window is still. Now I have the impression that something will break. Another heaving force pushes against the window, almost bending the glass. Perhaps I should have left some room to man-oeuvre. Taut substance is more brittle. But then I fall asleep and the subconscious gale blows itself out.

When my father went out to work the next morning he found broken slates on the doorstep. He took it almost as a personal affront. That was a dreadful storm last night. The wind almost had a malicious nature. He could have been walking out the door that very moment. The way I got the story, filtering through the half-dream as I got dressed, he might have been killed. That kind of thing is very dangerous.

My mother repeated the words after him as she went to look at the damage. It sounded much more dangerous coming from her in German.

'Das kann enorm gefärlich sein,' she said, seeing the broken slates. It could have sliced someone in the neck. Or it could have chopped someone's shoulder. Or imagine if somebody got that on his head.

'Jemand konnte das auf den kopf kriegen.' *Jemand*, somebody. The only person going out at that time was my father. Besides, the slates had fallen during the night. The morning was calm and seemed to promise a summer's day. There was no danger. The damage began to reduce from what seemed like three or four slates at first down to one grey slate broken into many pieces.

You couldn't leave a thing like that, even for a day. My father came back in and phoned Mr McNally. He wanted it fixed immediately. He could have phoned him from the office. But there was no time to waste in a situation like that. And Mr McNally, taking it to be a major job, agreed to set everything else aside.

My father was reassured. He picked up his briefcase containing the flask and the sandwiches, the two or three library books, and his copy of the *Irish Press* and set off to catch the train. Before he departed, he left my mother with a final command not to let the children out or at least to make sure they didn't stand under the falling slates.

By the time Mr McNally arrived, I had already had my breakfast and was at my desk in my room. I was studying for the Leaving Cert. It wasn't so much the act of pertinent study. It was more like trying to reduce the feeling of wasted months and wasted years. Hours or even minutes spent away from the books produced guilt and panic. The hounding force of Christian Brothers kept me in my room. There wasn't a minute to waste.

Mr McNally was talking to my mother in the hall. Coming from Kempen in Germany, my mother always had a healthy distrust of Irish workers. She was gentle and discreet. She knew the moods and mind-games that predicted the results. She understood the code under which Irish people worked. It was the spirit of 1916 which burned inside each person still. Her own husband was a fervent Nationalist. She knew that her German accent commanded respect. Her naïve and innocent enquiries got the work done. But you had to watch them, she always said.

'Scharf aufpassen,' are her words. Sharp is a great word in any language. My mother is very sharp when it comes to work.

Mr McNally was no exception. He fixed the roofs on a lot of the houses in Spencer Villas. Whether he was recommended or just happened to be in the right place at the right time was never clear. He didn't have a bad reputation anyway. Mrs Tarleton, the small Protestant woman next door in No. 1, occasionally asked Mr McNally to do the roof for her too. But she didn't trust him any more than my mother did. She used to follow Mr McNally up on to the roof to inspect his work personally. She was seventy, stooped and had bow legs. Mrs Tarleton trusted nobody. Not even us next door. Least of all us in No. 2.

Mr McNally always came and went and worked in the same grey suit. Grey as slate, I suppose. A thin man with a broad forehead. His hair must have been curly once because it now clung tightly to his head like a silver, corrugated bathing cap.

He always reminded me of President Nixon. He was a bit older than Nixon but a lot of the caricatures in magazines and newspapers fitted him just as well. Except that Mr McNally had a more honest face. He didn't look cunning.

But then Nixon didn't look cunning until the truth was out.

My mother treated an innocent face with great caution, but what she viewed with even more unqualified distrust was any hint of charm. A man with charm must have something to hide. A man with charm is up to something. Charm and innocence have always been incriminating traits and never worked on her. Mr McNally, as a person, was not without charm either.

'Good morning. Isn't it a magnificent day today?' My mother accepted it as a fact with a long 'Yes, it is.' 'Would you believe it, after such a storm last night?' he added. 'There's a lot of slates down this morning, I can tell you. Well, I suppose I better go up and make sure your roof stays on,' he said with a short laugh as he climbed the stairs in front of her.

To get to the roof, you had to go through a skylight into the attic and straight on through another skylight. It was awkward because you had to stand on the ladder and push the first skylight aside with both hands. I was called to help Mr McNally set up the ladder. He secured it against the banisters with a worn piece of nautical string. My mother was standing by. Her presence, if not providing an eager incentive to work, dispelled at least any obverse intention to idle or waste time. As soon as Mr McNally had pushed aside the heavy skylight, she sent me back to my books. 'Mr McNally can manage on his own now.' 'Absolutely,' he replied, looking down the ladder. 'I know these houses like the back of my hand.'

I was in the same boat as Mr McNally. With no further cause to deviate, I returned to my room. He disappeared too after two or three trips up and down the ladder. He explained what had to be done and my mother went downstairs to leave him to it.

Apart from suspicion, one of the sharpest weapons my

mother always had was her highly developed sense of smell. Her nose was very sensitive and she was quite proud of it. We knew it well, even if Mr McNally didn't. I can smell trouble, she would say. I can smell mischief. When we were young, we never doubted the unnatural powers of her fine, long nose.

Suspicion was her way of maintaining order in a large family. Whenever something was up she would look into your eyes and suspect a whole list of crimes to which you answered no each time until she suspected the right one. The silence would confirm it. And you could never tell a lie in a situation like that because she could smell a lie.

One day, when I had stolen a bar of chocolate in Hanahoe's shop, I was almost proud of myself underneath the guilt and terror. I knew I hadn't been seen. There was never any supervision in Hanahoe's. But you could never hide anything in the house so I put the chocolate under a bucket in the garden. I was too tense to eat any of it. When I met her in the kitchen, she knelt down to my level on her hunkers. She asked me straight out if I had stolen something. She couldn't have known. But all I could do was to stare down at her long straight nose and at her two rounded knees and admit. From there on, I had learned an eternal respect for that intelligent faculty of smell. When we grew older, of course, we realized that if you were accused of something you hadn't done, she was bluffing, and you might get away with a white lie. But never where it mattered. Even still, sometimes she appears unexpectedly at the door of my room.

The houses in Spencer Villas are terraced, red-brick houses with Georgian-type fanlights and bay windows to the front. The roofs are all connected from Nos. 1 to 15. This was one of the things that gave rise to the strongest suspicion with my mother. The fact that Mr McNally mended the roofs for other neighbours on the terrace meant that he could easily go up through our skylight and do somebody else's work at the same time.

In fact, she strongly suspected that Mr McNally was also doing a job for Mrs Tarleton next door. He could easily be using good slates from our roof to mend other jobs. But anything beyond the ladder and the skylight remained a collection of notions and suspicions in her imagination. Unlike Mrs Tarleton, she had never actually been up there herself.

My older brother and I knew far more about it. We had been up there a few times and knew the landscape well. Two Toblerone-shaped grey roofs stretched all the way down to the end. They were marked into sections by chimney stacks. In between was the part they called the valley. On a few occasions, we walked all the way along the valley right down to No. 15. With the chimneys at the end of each house, we were able to keep count, calling out the names on the way: Ryans, Richardsons, Beakys all the way down to Beddys. Over the front hump, if you climbed up from the valley, you could see the other side of the street, and the wider, vertiginous view of the bay and of Howth. Over the back, you saw the gardens, trees and surrounding hills. It was an ethereal place. Like being on top of a mountain.

After an hour or so, my mother came up the stairs and stopped at the bottom of the ladder. She called up the ladder to Mr McNally and said she had a cup of tea ready for him. It was the only excuse she had and the only way she could monitor the progress of his work. The risk of allowing deception to carry on unnoticed far outweighed the risk of good work briefly interrupted.

'Mr McNally,' she called again. But there was no response. She waited for an appropriate minute or two to see if he heard her. She waited long enough to dispel any hint of impatience. Then she called again. In the outlines of her German accent, his name sounded more like Mr McNelly.

'Mr McNelly,' she called up through the skylight. Again she paused, so as not to be discourteous.

'Mr McNelly, I have a cup of tea ready for you.' The word 'tea' had emphasis.

There was no reaction. She called a few more times at long intervals and then gave it up. She deduced that he must have climbed out of the valley, out of earshot, on to the outer slopes of the roof. Dangerous place. He was obviously busy. So she went downstairs again and left him alone.

She left it for another half an hour before she came back up again. Once more she stood at the bottom of the ladder, wishing that her fears would only allow her to climb up through the skylight herself.

'Mr McNelly,' she called and then waited to see if he would appear.

A strong beam of sunshine came down through the skylight, making her wince as she looked up. The sun shone through my window as well, projecting a thin, disfigured frame on to the floor of the room. It was a liquid beam full of floating particles.

'Mr McNelly, I have your tea ready now.' She waited quietly. She called twice more but there was no answer. Perhaps his hearing wasn't so good. Perhaps he was still on the outer slopes of the roof. Her calls abated and she went back downstairs again. A little while later I heard her calling from outside in the back garden.

'Mr McNelly.' I heard it clearly through the window. Surely Mr McNally had heard it too? She walked right down to the end of the garden and looked up to see if she could spot him. She called again from there. Allowing that reasonable gap for response, she went back inside. The back door closed with a familiar clap.

She walked up through the hallway to the front door and opened it.

'Mr McNelly,' she called from the front garden this time. The name and her accent echoed along the terrace. Then I heard her calling him again, but more faintly than before; perhaps from out on the street or the pavement. A slight breeze began to rush through the house. It rushed and sucked from the skylight right down to the front door. It rushed lightly down along the beam of sunlight, down the stairs, through the hallway and, catching the door gently, slammed it shut.

Moments later the doorbell rang and I went down to let her in. She said she was sorry to have taken me away from my study. She explained her difficulty locating Mr McNally. I suggested that he was probably working on something and that he might be best left to it. I went back to my room. She went back into the kitchen.

But very soon she was back up again and once again calling Mr McNally through the skylight. It seemed as though she was calling a celestial spirit. Under the bright beam of sunshine, shielding her eyes, her appellation seemed to be directed at the Almighty.

'Mr McNelly . . . Mr McNelly.' But nothing worked. Her prayers went unheeded and nobody appeared in the skylight.

Eventually she called me instead and asked me to go up the ladder and take a look. She said she was worried that something might have happened to Mr McNally. He wasn't that young either.

Of course I was very happy to be given a decent reason to escape from study but I was less happy to be the instrument of her suspicion. I knew very well that she wanted to catch him out. I asked her if it was not better to leave him up there until he finished his work. I told her if he didn't do his job properly she didn't have to pay him. But that was all irrelevant. She said she was concerned about him.

She insisted. I climbed the ladder along the sunbeam towards the skylight. I was very reluctant to be seen as an inspector – the sting of her suspicion emerging through the skylight. No matter how much she claimed to understand the Irish worker, I claimed to know him better. The one thing he really hates is to be checked up on.

It was very hot on the roof. I was blinded with the sunshine and saw nothing at first. I searched the slopes and saw the shape of Mr McNally, lying back at an angle of 45 degrees against the roof, asleep with his hands behind his head. He must have been two or three houses down from ours. I coughed and he woke up, looking all around him. Then he saw me and got up to walk towards me, dusting himself off.

'Ah, there you are,' he said, almost in chant. 'All finished now.'

Mad Dog

Liz waited at the corner of Clare Street on the Greene's bookshop side. Had she known about the noise, she would have met Maurice somewhere else. The street was saturated by the profane sound of a pneumatic drill being operated by a workman on the opposite side. The noise was so strong it covered everything else. People hurried past that point on Clare Street as though they were embarrassed. The traffic was silent. Coming from Merrion Square, two buses floated through the wide junction past the traffic lights and came to rest at the bookshop. A blue car floated after them.

She looked around for Maurice but he didn't appear anywhere. She became instinctively impatient as though Maurice was hours late. The noise across the street made her intolerant and she began to rip up the pavement along with the drill. A man with bony arms and rippling muscles controlled the direction with his hands and stomach leaning heavily on the drill. But the bouncing made him look lighter than the drill. It gave him light bones. A tattoo above his elbow quivered. The drill itself had two large nostrils through which a powerful rhythmic exhaust was emitted. Every now and then, the street would shed a layer of sound as the man lifted the drill with hands and stomach and forced it, impatiently, into another unbroken part of the pavement. In those intervals, the sound of traffic came back like an aviary.

Then the noise froze the air again. Every muscle in the man's body fought to control the new, more satisfactory destruction. Other workers moved in behind him with shovels. The noise oppressed her and she couldn't trust her hearing, like wildlife around airports, momentarily deaf and defenceless when a jet takes off. Anything could give her a fright. When she was clutched from behind by the shoulders and given a kiss on the cheek, she had to turn around and face him before she could be sure it was Maurice.

'Jesus, Morry, where were you? I'm nearly deaf with the noise,' she shouted.

'I can't hear you, I'm deaf,' he shouted back pointing in the direction of the drill. He turned her round, putting his arm around her shoulder, and they walked away quickly into the artificial silence of Nassau Street. They could hear the drilling going on in the distance behind them, like a bell. She was still impatient.

'That was a great place you picked to meet me. My ears are ringing.'

'How was I to know?' he retorted smiling.

'Where are we going for lunch?'

'Well, I was thinking of taking you to Pizzaworld up in Grafton Street. We've never been there. There's only one problem though. I've no money.'

'Don't look at me,' she said pivoting her head round to see his eyes. 'The only money I have, I have to keep for my parents' anniversary gift.'

'Don't worry! I've got a great plan. We're going to do a mad dog. For the crack. Have you ever done it before?'

'I did not! The only thing I ever did was to walk past the cashier in Bewley's without paying.'

'Fair play to you! It's quite simple anyhow. We'll just sit somewhere close to the door and I'll let you run out first.'

'Thanks very much!'

Ever since September, when Liz began to take her secretarial course, they had had lunch together almost every day. They had tried almost every restaurant, café, snack bar, delicatessen and pub in the city and still Maurice came up with new places to go. He was original like that. It was he who found the Civil Service dining-hall, full of crusty old civil servants and clerks and nuns too. The food was really cheap and there was lots to laugh at. Then he found the Legion of Mary soup kitchen down around Holles Street where they went once for the laugh.

Some days, they would just get sandwiches or buy food so that they could have it on the grass in Trinity. If Maurice's boss was out for lunch, they could have it there in the office. Tomatoes, scallions, mayonnaise, chives, cheese, olives and even chocolate biscuits. What was left over would be kept by Maurice in his drawer till it went off. They had great arguments about sardines which were the only thing she hated and which he ate with unreserved relish. She called them 'sourdeens' and warned him that she would not kiss him if he defied her by eating them. Sometimes she sat, and watched quietly while he ate a whole tin of anchovies without a word.

Once, she stepped up on Maurice's desk, cleared the remainder of the food with her foot and began to dance, even feigning a striptease by showing him her legs and her breasts. It was enough to give his desk and the whole environment of the Speedofreight offices a sense of unease for weeks afterwards.

They were an unusual couple. That went without saying. It was only when she met one of her schoolfriends that somebody would actually say it. Nothing they did was ever remotely conventional. Even the way in which they first met on the bus on her way to school. She had seen him getting on the same bus for months till one day she got the nerve with her friend Maureen to sit next to him. 'Why don't you take us out for a drink sometime?' she said to him. He turned out to be four years older than her. The whole thing became a scandal in school which made her feel even more unique. Within a few weeks, she felt she knew Maurice so well that she told him straight out that she couldn't wait to sleep with him. Her mind was made up. He was one in a million.

By the time the scandal, fed on morsels of information passed on by Maureen, had a chance to grow out of proportion, the final leaving exams had come and gone and Liz had already left school. They were travelling down the dual carriageway in a van borrowed by Maurice when she finally knew that at this point, her real life was beginning. She even said it out loud in her mind. From then on, everything they said, everything they saw or spoke was unique. Everything they did became a story.

The van broke down in one of the most remote and bleak spots in the middle of the country. They didn't care. When it was too late to get a mechanic, they just found a nearby pub and sat talking all evening. Self-contained! When the pub closed they reeled back along the pitch-black road together, laughing and threatening to push each other into the ditch, almost passing the spot where the van was parked and finally settling into their sleeping bags on the foam mattress in the back of the van where they fell into a capsule of scented sleep together.

By lunchtime when they awoke, they were both so hungry that they immediately began to eat their sandwiches and milk in the van. Later they walked to the village again and found a mechanic. By afternoon, they were ready to forsake that bleak spot in the middle of nowhere which they had made so important in their sleep. An unmarked shrine of evaporated love by the roadside. It would take a hundred years before something important would ever happen at that spot again: a fatal crash or a murder or a house built or the road itself widened.

That evening, not long after the sun had gone, they caught the first sight of the calm, windless Atlantic as they came over a hill on the road. It disappeared again for a while as they drove on down the hill and reappeared as they reached the shore. There they took in a sight which was to become a symbol of their time together. A pictorial title for a collection of impressions. She had the feeling once more that this is where her real life was about to begin.

They travelled around Clare mostly along the coast with no further plan than to make their way gradually up to Galway where she would pay a brief visit to her grand-mother. They met all kinds of people. They picked up hitchhikers and met a group of Germans with whom they spent an evening in a pub in Kildysert. They also met a well-known piper who brought them to a pub in Lahinch and told them all about his life, the details of his broken marriage and his endless travels. He only played his instrument with great reluctance when asked to play a fourth time by Liz. They met old men in the pubs who argued about politics and love. Some of them with caps and threadbare jackets and dental flaws which gave them a cartoon perfection. Old men with boyish faces, custodians of premonition and sadness who sang songs about emigration and broken-hearted maidens and sailors returning after years on the sea clutching half of a ring and searching for the unrecognizable woman who possessed the other half of the same ring. Often, Liz got the feeling that everything they said or sang about had something to do with herself and Maurice too. She could see herself and Maurice as figures in any one of those songs. In that way they were not so much unique but fitted a classical formula of lovers. Now and again, she even recognized parts of Maurice in some of the old men. The way he approached a pint of Guinness or shrugged his shoulders was similar. She enjoyed nothing more than to watch them look at a pint, look away, look back at the pint, alter position at the bar and lift the pint to take a gulp.

They argued with some of those men too. Some jovially. Some in earnest. And Maurice held his own always, overturning preconceived ideas in his own unique way of arguing. He could sidestep any issue. One evening, a man introduced himself by asking a riddle and then sat down beside Liz from where he sang songs and talked to her all night while Maurice was being ignored. It was the first time she had ever noticed jealousy in him. It seemed ridiculous, he said later, but he formed the impression that she would never belong to him but to whoever was talking to her, or whatever occupied her mind at any particular time. She had to remind him when they lay down together in the back of the van that this is what really counted and told her she was really alive. She couldn't say what else was on her mind; that she had begun to compare everyone she met with Maurice.

One morning when they awoke from their embrace, they found a word which was to become the official word for their trip along the coast together. A word that fitted everything. It came from a political argument in the pub the previous night. A man had come forward after drinking in silence for a long time and told them what he felt about Patrick Pearse and 1916. 'Died for nothing,' he said. 'All those people who died for Ireland, died for nothing. Look at all this caper up in the North now. I'm telling you, they died for nothing.' His sentences were short and became shorter as the night went on. In the end, he became very drunk and continued to repeat himself with a sullen, drunken look. 'Died for nothing! Died for nothing! All this caper! Died for nothing! For Nothing . . . for nothing.' He kept repeating it as if some of his companions in the pub were about to carry him home and change his mind.

When they remembered the word in the morning, they both fell about laughing.

'What's all this caper?' Maurice asked, while sorting out his tangled clothes. They laughed till they were almost exhausted. They always woke up giddy and hungry. Then Maurice would say the word again and send them both into further fits of laughing.

'Cut out that caper,' he demanded when she was blowing her nose noisily.

Later on when they were buying some food in a small supermarket, it was Liz who recalled the word saying: 'I want none of your caper with sourdeens now!' At that, they stumbled around the shop in bursts of suppressed sniggers which were acknowledged with a suppressed smile or more like a trace of gastric pain by the woman on the cash register.

Each day they moved somewhere new. A collection of events along their trip to the west of Ireland had become compiled into that first sight of the ocean. Whenever Liz thought about Maurice and herself, it was never without that solid image of the motionless coast. Ever since then she had become aware of a developing impatience at anything ugly or anything which refused to match that scene. Not an offensive impatience but a feeling that she couldn't wait for things to begin.

As they walked along Nassau Street on this mild October day, they could appreciate the quiet signs of lunchtime.

Everyone stopped to look at things. People glanced at magazines they would never buy. They had time to make comparisons between sandwiches. As always, somebody had stopped along the railings of Trinity College to look at the athletics or the hockey match. Liz felt Maurice's hand on her neck as he led the way beside her. It was almost the same grip with which you would duck someone's head under water, but she trusted it. His hand at the base of her neck was so reassuring and almost suave that it concealed all malice. Like everything else, it was their own special way of walking together. Their invention.

In the restaurant, they sat two tables back from the door and the wide glass windows where Liz could watch the people passing by outside. Maurice sat facing in where he could see the waitress. Two tables further down sat two nuns reading and talking about the litany of pizzas on the menu. Maurice found himself calculating. There were three yards between Liz and the door. There were six yards between Liz and the waitress.

'Look at those nuns there,' Liz said when she saw them. 'Aren't they having a great time these days?'

'Ah sure, fair play to them,' he answered half in a Clare accent.

'They're probably going for a few pints later.' Liz sniggered.

When the waitress arrived to take their order, Maurice and Liz were still searching the menu and she stared out at the pedestrians as if expecting someone in particular to pass by.

Liz said she would order the pizza Napoli. 'Is that very big?' she asked the waitress who answered that there were only two sizes: large and small. Maurice ordered a pizza with everything and was told there were no anchovies. As an afterthought, he ordered two glasses of red wine. The waitress wrote the docket, placed it between salt and pepper and folded up the menu cards without a word, still keeping a half-interested eye on the street outside.

'What's yours like?' Maurice asked when they had begun to eat.

'It's lovely, have a taste.' They swapped portions of pizza and ate without further comment. When Maurice was almost finished he said it was just basically like melted cheese and tomato ketchup on toast.

'It's a rip-off,' he said and Liz told him to be quiet at least till she was finished.

The waitress came and took the plates with the same lack of interest as before and brought two coffees which she added on to the bill before replacing it again between salt and pepper. Maurice said he would never come here again. Liz laughed without making any sound. Maurice quickly gave a running commentary on the eating habits of nuns. Then he saw the manager, a thin man with glasses at the back of the restaurant. Liz asked if they were really going to go through with it and Maurice answered: of course. He couldn't allow any doubt. The plan was final. It was every man for himself, he explained, and he would meet her in ten minutes at the bottom of Grafton Street.

That was the moment it began. Liz saw Maurice give her the nod and she got up from the table. She hooked her bag on to her shoulder and walked casually over to the door. From that moment on, her actions seemed like part of one enlarged movement. She opened the door slowly as if to emphasize that she was in no rush. As always when she walked out of a room with people, she was suddenly aware that somebody might be looking at her bottom. She stepped out on to the pavement and turned up the street. Only when she heard Maurice's command right behind her close to her ear, 'run for it', did she break into a sprint. She had often heard him say things into her ear like that from behind when she was half asleep in bed.

She ran through the pedestrians wherever she could find gaps. Everything followed like a programmed movement. Once she left the table in the restaurant, it was all consecutive like a stone on its way to a window.

She turned into the lane after a few yards as planned. Neither of them could remember the name of the lane except that it was called 'something Court'. She couldn't think of anything now. She was travelling too fast to think. The only thing she felt as she turned into the lane was something under her left foot which was unmistakably someone else's foot. A few yards further on, she almost fell right over a child in a buggy.

Maurice had taken a different route as a decoy. Spotting an opportune gap in the pedestrian traffic, he ran headlong into Duke Street opposite the restaurant.

It seemed to Liz that people at lunchtime had slowed down to a standstill. Her shoulder bag kept bouncing against her. People became obstacles. She had to avoid them and run around them all the way along this lane of shops. When she came to the end she was out of breath. With the force of exhaustion, she convinced herself that she was out of danger. That single action which began by standing up from the table now slowed down to a stroll. Just look normal, she told herself as she turned down Clarendon Street. This street was quiet and had few pedestrians.

Gradually, her slower pace allowed her to think again. Where was Maurice? Was he caught? And then she began to get a peculiar feeling that she herself was being followed. She looked behind her instinctively and saw somebody walking behind her. For an instant she thought it was Maurice. But she realized immediately that it wasn't. She was being followed. Or was it a mere coincidence that somebody happened to be walking down the same street? She had to stop herself from hurrying her pace.

She couldn't look around again because it would attract suspicion. She wanted to run but had to remain normal and casual. She wanted to sit down on the pavement to get her breath back but she couldn't do that either. She was aware that she had run away with a meal in her stomach that didn't belong to her. Her body still followed the same trajectory which urged her feet, her knees and her eyes on to the end of Clarendon Street where she could turn the corner and run again. She became impatient at the pavement which passed so slowly underneath her. She was impatient with her own footsteps.

Her footsteps were then overshadowed and doubled by a person walking right behind her. Her walk had become mingled with that behind her and then she felt a sudden magnetic pull on her left shoulder.

'Hold on there now!' she heard. Without a second thought, Liz stopped and turned with automatic anger.

'What do you think you're doing? Let go of me,' she demanded. It was all her breath would allow her to say with confidence. A man with glasses now stood before her holding her shoulder. She felt herself being pushed back against the wall. The glasses seemed to emphasize his eyes. As if the eyes belonged to a much larger, much angrier person. He wasn't much taller than Maurice. His nose seemed quite flat, unlike Maurice's. Liz knew he was serious and meant business.

'I'll tell you what I'm doing.' He stopped for breath. 'I want you to pay for your meal back there, or else I'll get the Guards.' His face was only inches away from hers. They were both breathing together and looking straight into each other's eyes. There was a pause in which she almost thought she was looking at Maurice.

'I'm telling you,' the man in front of her repeated, 'I'm serious. I want eight pounds and forty-five pence from you. I know it was you 'cos I followed you.'

There was no point. She was caught and looking straight into the manager's eyes. His eyes seemed more and more out of proportion to the rest of his face, as if his anger had enlarged them. His chest, still working rapidly, seemed to belong to a weaker, more timid person. His shirt and tie belonged to a far more substantial man. His voice was borrowed from a teacher or a trade unionist. Liz felt embarrassed and hot. But she didn't want to concede. She didn't allow herself to feel betrayed or let down and what she said after a brief pause was as natural as blinking or brushing her hair back.

'Now I understand. Look, I'm terribly sorry about this, I really am. You see, my boyfriend and I had a terrible argument and I don't know where he went. Of course I'll pay you. We both seem to have forgotten completely about the bill.'

The moment she said it, she was convinced it was true. The man in front of her just kept staring at her without another word. She looked down and began to take the purse from her bag and said:

'Please let go of my shoulder.'

Goodbye to the Hurt Mind

You're full a shite . . . he said, looking straight over at me.

When you hear that coming in a slick Belfast accent, there's no mistake. Nobody was looking for trouble. Nobody had said a word to him. He seemed very drunk and his dark eyes looked across at me either with intense rage or intense stupor.

I said nothing. I half knew the woman he was with, Helen Connors. She looked at him reproachfully, and frowned at the floor beneath him. Graham, she pleaded. What are you saying? He was drunk; slumped down on his elbows. But he kept staring up at me. We were all sitting at this large round table listening to the band playing. His eyes wouldn't leave me. The candle at the centre of the table seemed to make everything look darker. It cast a black wavering circular shadow beneath itself on the table. Gave Helen Connors a black line for her cleavage. Even the wine looked black in the glasses; black as H-block flags or black plastic bags. And candles seem to give everyone such pale flesh-tones, like degraded election posters gone pale with age. The music was just about loud enough to pretend nothing was happening.

Full a shite . . . he repeated.

How long can you ignore that? I looked away; pretended to be desperately interested in the band at that moment. But you can't ignore it. Because you then begin to think, maybe he's half right. Maybe he knows something.

The Belfast accent keeps ringing in your ear. It's like tinnitus. You can never be sure either what they're saying up there. Was it 'shite' or 'shout' he said? By the sound of it, so many words seem interchangeable in Northern Ireland. Paisley used to shout a lot. Twice, I've been up there for a bit of fishing and they all keep shouting about Fashion . . . fashion . . . fashion.

I couldn't help taking another look at your man from Belfast, but he was still staring at me. Why me? I thought. Beside the candle on the table there was a blue menu card jammed between pepper and salt and a small vase containing a single daffodil. This was repeated on every table.

Janet asked me to collect her mother from the hairdresser. Her mother always pretends at the hairdresser's that I am her lover. Here's my Romeo, she says. I wait in the cane chairs without picking up one of the magazines on the glass table. They offer me coffee. No thanks! The mirrors are also framed with cane. The image must have been decided on from the beginning; cane surrounds along with red towels. I can half see Janet's mother's face in the mirror. Somebody sweeps up the cut hair around her on the floor. There is an ad on the radio for late-night shopping. The oval mirror is held to the back of Janet's mother's head and the back of the head must go nodding into infinity along the mirrors. I have to remember to tell her that her hair looks great. Janet's mother links arms as we leave the hairdresser's and the girls smile. The scent of hairspray fills the car.

Helen Connors was the first to make a move. She stood up and put her coat on. Then gave Belfast a slap on the shoulder with the back of her hand and said: Come on you. Treats him like a schoolboy. Up you get! He is footless;

makes the bar look like a ferry. She left him propped for a moment against a chair while she plunged down towards us to pick up her bag, looking at me with a half-smile before she steered him out through the gaps in the tables, past the stage and through the door out into the street.

As soon as he was gone, they started talking about him. They said he was manky. Mouldy. Out of it. Somebody told me he worked as a photographer. Not long after that, I left as well and my ears were buzzing when I stepped out into the street. When I got home, the house seemed unusually quiet. In the kitchen, the sandwiches and flasks stood ready for school in the morning. I sat down and switched the radio on and refused to think about the next day. I knew Janet was already half way through it.

The next time I saw Helen Connors, she was standing naked in a field beside a tree. There was another photograph of her sitting naked in a large empty room looking straight at you through an open door. There was no mistake; it was Helen Connors without her clothes on. I recognized her immediately. His name was there too: Graham Delargy. The rest of the photographs in the exhibition were of helicopters or soldiers or walls with graffiti.

I had never imagined Helen Connors like that with dusty circular shadings around her nipples and I couldn't look at her any longer because breasts are like eyes, bogus eyes. So I walked around looking at other pictures. But when I came back to her, there were two women examining her.

Nobody likes repetition. Why can't things happen just once?

When Janet's mother comes around to dinner on Tuesdays, she wears her fur coat. She likes to pretend this is a special occasion, her first ever visit to the house. I hand her a glass of sherry. She takes my arm and says to Janet: You don't mind if I borrow your husband for a moment? Janet's mother tells me about a famous dentist she could have married. He was mad about her. Extremely intelligent man. He asked her to marry him many times but she turned him down. Gave him back the ring he once gave her; they were on the train at the time going from Limerick to Dublin when he accepted the ring back and then threw it out the window of the carriage.

Why didn't she marry him? I ask. But she can't answer that. Usually people want to know if she remembered the spot where he threw the ring out. Did anyone go back to look for it? She laughs. That was an expensive ring, too.

After dinner, Janet asks me to put on a waltz for her mother. Dancing rinses out resentment, her mother says. She likes 'The Blue Danube' best. She once stayed in Vienna. It was in Vienna that she learned to dance. Mere contact with the city was enough – *Einmal hin, einmal her, rund herum, das ist nicht schwer*. Janet's mother wants me to dance with her. I'm much taller than she is. But not firm enough. Too stiff. Too stiff. Ah, you're no use at all, she says. A man should lead. Are you a man?

Janet dances with one of the children. Their movements are exaggerated and comic. This is a repetition of last week.

I was bound to meet him again at some stage. Delargy. When I did, some months later on one of those fishing trips up north, it was a bit of a shock. I had no idea who else was going on the trip and we both happened to be invited by the same people; mutual friends. He was introduced to me as Graham Delargy and we had to pretend we had never met before.

From first eye contact there seemed to be an unspoken arrangement between us not to bring up anything from the past. I had to pretend I didn't know he was a photographer. I had to laugh and respond to his conversation like any new acquaintance. He had to ensure he didn't appear to be apologetic or considerate. When he held the door of the bar open for me, it had to appear natural as though he would have done it for any stranger. When I bought him a pint, he quickly bought one back at the next opportunity so as to keep a surface equality. And of course we couldn't say a word about Helen Connors.

Next morning on the way down to the lake from the lodging-house, things seemed less strained; less like a conspiracy. There was the weather to talk about, and fishing conditions. You get on better with declared opponents than you do with declared friends. When I got into the same boat with him and accidentally pushed against him, it almost appeared as though I had finally decided to take revenge and push him into the lake. Out on the lake, it's every man for himself. There's not much to talk about anyway. Anglers are solipsists. There was the irrational anxiety that hooks and lines would become entangled. And later, I reached for a sandwich in my bag and discovered it was his bag I was fumbling at and quickly withdrew my hand.

In the bar that evening, everybody got drunk. Delargy more than anyone. We were getting on very well. Then, as if to wipe the slate clean, Delargy put his arm around one of the other anglers who happened to be talking too much and said: You're full a shite – you scabby bastard. Inverse flattery. It's the way angling friends are in Ireland; insulted if you stop insulting them. The way a fish would feel insulted if you didn't eat it after you went and caught it.

Janet likes to repeat things. She can relate the same story twice or three times over in successive phone calls. When I read a book, I hold it so that it looks almost unread when

I'm finished. Janet cracks the spine and leaves books face down on the sofa while she's on the phone.

Janet remembers odd things. Names of people and street names. She still knows the name of the shopkeeper at the end of the road in Wood Green when we lived in London. He was from Pakistan. I'd have to ask her. She still knows the names of all the streets around there and all the names on the bells of each flat in the house. I remember the up-turned ice cream cone beneath the seat of the bus the day we went to visit her uncle. She could tell me the name of the pub we drank in. The Elephant and Castle?

Janet hates bringing the car to the garage for repairs. She says it reminds her of a gynaecological examination every time a mechanic starts poking around underneath the bonnet. Janet never remembers to check the oil in the car because that's something I remember.

It is me who collects the car from the garage in the afternoon. It is me who first grips the oily steering wheel when I get into the car. It is the mechanic who sees me searching for tissues and points knowingly to a large drum of blotting paper on the wall. It is both Janet and her mother who are at the hairdresser's today. It is me who remembers to say that they both have lovely hair.

Long after Janet's mother is gone home again, Janet asks me if I remember the name of a pub in Kensington. I ask her if she knows the colours of Lufthansa. She asks if I know the name of the bakery on the High Street. I ask her what date internment was introduced. What is the capital of Fiji? Who was the bass guitarist with the Rolling Stones?

It is me who lies in bed awake and cannot avoid remembering the name of the garage: Huet Motors. I continually see petrol pumps and the greasy interior of the workshop. It is me who thinks the bed is on the floor of the workshop. It is Janet who embraces me.

Mind you don't get any oil on my hair.

There's nothing in the world but the thought in my head.

The last time I met him was outside Trinity College, along the railings. It must have been around five o'clock in the evening. People were going home from work. The windows of passing buses were steamed up. The passengers upstairs had cleared circles with the sleeves of their coats; enough to look out at the street and the railings of Trinity and the people walking by. Delargy stopped me and asked me what I was doing. I can never describe what I'm doing.

Come on you bugger, he said. Let's murder a pint.

On our way to the pub, we passed lots of people waiting for buses. As usual, there was a man selling the evening papers at the corner of Westmoreland Street. As usual, I remember the names of streets when I pass through them and forget them again as soon as they are behind me.

He told me he was getting out. Australia. He had organized a job over there in Sydney.

You bastard!

There was a mate of his already over there with a house on a beach near the city.

You dirty bastard!

In the pub he kept talking about Australia. Fishing. Hunting. Women. Dynamite. From time to time I had to look at my watch. It's goodbye to Ireland, he kept saying. Goodbye to the hurt mind. Then he ordered more and more pints so that we lost count. Come on, let's make a disgrace of ourselves, he said.

The barman kept laughing at him. Told him to make sure and put on a condom when he got off the plane in Sydney, like a good lad.

I had to carry him home. He kept shouting and mumbling. In the door of Burger King, he shouted: Goodbye to the hurt mind, but there was no reaction except a few puzzled stares.

As we arrived around at Helen Connors's house, he fell asleep on her doorstep. He couldn't even make it into the hallway. I had to pretend I had never seen her body naked before. I had to pretend everything was a surprise. We carried him in and laid him on the bed. I took off his boots. She took off his jacket.

A Third – A Third – A Third

When times were good, they had the central heating put in. The night the plumber, Leo Stanley, came around with the estimate, they brought him in to sit by the fire like a guest. She even offered to make tea. There was talk about 'a turd – a turd – and a turd' which nobody understood at first. And Leo Stanley seemed uncomfortable sitting down discussing money so he stood up and began to describe the system he would install. He emphasized the extra water pressure they wanted in the shower with a downturned hand pouring chubby fingers straight down over the carpet. He told them not to rush into it. 'Tink it over,' he said as he left quietly, leaving behind his big lips and his big smile.

But they had already made up their minds. So they went upstairs and had a bath together. When they got into bed, they made love and she even did something she hadn't done in a long time. She heard him shout as if he was expecting an echo to come back from another part of the house; from downstairs or from outside in the street where sometimes on Friday or Saturday nights they heard random sounds of voices. She felt his knee twitching a few times. With the side of her head resting on his chest she felt she was listening to a cistern or a copper cylinder. Before she went to sleep, she wanted to say something but she found it hard to speak because her lips were big and numb. She couldn't pronounce the R in his name.

'Derek . . . I'm really glad we're getting it done. Aren't you?'

Two weeks later when Leo Stanley arrived to begin the job, she was there to open the door. She was interested in everything. She loved the sound of the copper pipes and watched him carry them in and place them along the floor in the hall. He spoke a bit like a priest and whenever she asked questions, he politely explained everything with his fingers, now and then making a copper pipe out of his index finger. He worked quietly. She made him tea. Occasionally, they met on the stairs and they would both stand back to let the other pass. But his courtesy always won. 'Fire ahead,' he insisted every time.

On the second day she asked him why he was putting black rubber tubes around the pipes.

'It protects the pipes, Mary,' he said. Then he gripped his index finger with his palm. 'It contains the heat and stops them from bursting too.'

Then with a slight stammer and a broad smile on his lips, he said: 'We call them, you know, prophylactics . . . in the trade, like.'

After that, she left him alone to work quietly for the rest of the week. Not wishing to be in his way too much, she took the baby out for long walks in the pram. When she got back, she would be delighted at the progress. Then she would hear him moving around upstairs or in the kitchen, whistling a tune; a well-known melody speeded up almost beyond recognition.

When the job was finished, he kept coming back to adjust things. The pilot light went out and he showed her how to relight it. He asked her to have a shower and to let him know if the pressure was right. He was professional about everything. And then one evening, he came around to collect his money: the second third. They had paid a third as a deposit. He said he could wait for a while for the last third, but he needed to be paid for the second third immediately.

They didn't have it. They explained that something had happened. So they offered to pay by the week instead. At first, he was extremely annoyed even though he remained polite as ever, and then he began to understand their predicament. Every Friday, for months, he arrived at the door to collect his weekly payment.

But in due course, even that stopped. They couldn't even afford that much. Leo Stanley would restrain himself and plead like a priest at the door.

' – Ah, you're letting me down, Mary.'

She pleaded too, saying that things had become so bad they couldn't even use the central heating any more.

'But look, Mary, I've lost money on this job. My materials are in there.'

She hated being in the house on Fridays when he called. She hated telling him there was nothing. At one time, she offered him her children's allowance which was far short of the right amount. But he wouldn't accept the few pounds.

' – Come on Mary. Who do you think I am?'

After that, he stopped coming. Some reminders came in the post threatening legal action. But they stopped as well. They couldn't understand why. About six months later, they met Leo Stanley – and his wife – by accident in a city-centre restaurant. It was Mary's birthday and they had to avoid eye contact with Leo Stanley throughout the meal. But eventually he came over anyhow and seemed very friendly. They explained laboriously that it was a special night out, celebrating her birthday. But they kept thinking that he was counting up the cost of the meal, the babysitter and the drinks afterwards. In the end, Leo Stanley said nothing about money at all.

Perhaps that was worse. From now on, they could go nowhere now that Leo Stanley seemed to be everywhere. They were confined to the house. When they got home that night, she got the impression that she had been out with Leo Stanley instead. In bed, while he placed his hand on her stomach and began to circle around slowly, she turned and said:

'Are you not embarrassed that we can't pay Leo Stanley?'

'Sure I am, but what can I do?'

She decided she was going to try and find work. A few weeks later, she did find something, teaching aerobics at the Lyndon Centre. But the occasional ten or twenty pounds she earned there soon became too precious to give away to Leo Stanley. And even that became embarrassing at times because Leo's wife attended the classes there. She looked very different in a bottle-green leotard, but Mary recognized her instantly. There was no escape, it seemed.

It must have been almost a year later when Mary met Leo Stanley again just when the whole thing was beginning to fade away at last. She was at the shopping centre, pushing her young daughter Emily in a buggy in front of her, when he appeared, coming almost directly towards her. She instinctively turned at an angle as though she remembered something and walked away towards the record shop. She heard him calling after her. But she didn't stop, pretending not to hear him. And then he came rushing after her and caught up with her, slightly panting as he spoke. He had changed. He had become a lot thinner but his lips were still as big as ever.

'Mary, can I talk to you sometime? I'm not talking about money now. I just want to talk to you about this new Herbaslim stuff. It's something you can make a lot of money out of.'

She was in no position to refuse. He bent down and winked at her daughter Emily, taking her small hand in his big tubular fingers. He continued to talk about Herbaslim. In her hurry to get away, she made the mistake of telling him to drop in at the house sometime.

'I'll guarantee you,' he said. 'You'll be interested. This stuff is amazing.'

When he arrived at the door a week later, he wore a grey suit which made him look a lot thinner and more serious than ever before. He was a different man. On his lapel, he wore a badge bearing the words: 'Want to be slim? Ask how.'

Without much enthusiasm, she asked him to come in and sit in the armchair. She thought of all the new things in the room since he was there last: the new wallpaper, the clock and the record player. She would like to have hidden them or explained that they were gifts from her mother. He noticed it too and told her she had the place looking very nice. Then he bent down to the little girl, Emily, and said: 'I met you when you were only a tiny, tiny baby.' He sat down and placed his briefcase on the floor beside him. It was obviously very new.

'Mary, I didn't come here to talk to you about money. I only want to talk to you about this Herbaslim stuff. This is what I would call something truly revolutionary.'

He produced a packet of Herbaslim from his briefcase.

' – Now you probably remember me being a bit on the fat side. Well, a bit overweight anyway.' She could neither agree nor disagree. So she said nothing.

'Thanks to this stuff, I look the way I am.' He stood up again to let her see. He reminded her more than ever of a Mormon missionary.

'Mary, I know you don't need this Herbaslim for yourself or anything, but don't you do a bit of the aerobics at the

Lyndon Centre? Well, you could make an absolute fortune selling these down there.'

He held the packet out, propped up on his fingers as if he were an art collector.

'The results you get from this are truly phenomenal.' He shook his head from side to side to emphasize the point. 'People don't know what's happening to them when they take this. I've seen people – you know, really obese women – slimming right down in three weeks. And still they're coming back for more. I made over a thousand pounds in the last month selling this.'

She asked him if he still worked at plumbing too.

'Ah yes. I still have the plumbing as well. But this is a real winner, I'll tell you. Let me explain.'

He stood up again and began to describe the function of the substance.

'You know they're all talking about fibre these days. Well this Herbaslim is one step up from all that fibre stuff. You see, it's really scientific. That's the beauty of it, Mary. All you do is take one glass of this stuff every day and you don't know yourself. They don't need fibre any more.'

He held out his hand to demonstrate, stretching out the fingers like a star.

'The way it is, Mary . . . your stomach is a bit like that. The food has to make its way through these tubes, right along, in and out.' He followed the course of the food in and out through his fingers.

'Now what this stuff does is it cleans you right out.' He demonstrated the clearance, pretending to push the food out, like dough stuck between the fingers.

'You see, these tubes in your stomach have little contractions all the time while you're digesting your dinner, like. That's what pushes the food on. But sometimes, these tubes get a bit lazy, you see, and that's when you need something like this Herbaslim to clean you out properly. And that's what slimming is about. There's nothing to it. Just a clean body.'

She thought of the U-bend of a toilet. To support his theory, Leo Stanley seemed to ascribe all his plumbing knowledge to the anatomy.

'Just think of it, Mary. If you were to sell these down at the Lyndon Centre, you could make a right little nest egg for yourself in no time. The women down there would love it. I'll guarantee you. I know, because my wife goes down there sometimes. But you need the aerobics teacher to recommend the stuff.'

How could she refuse to do it? She was staring money in the face, he told her. So she told him she would definitely think it over. After he was gone, she kept looking at the sample packet he had left behind on the mantelpiece for her. She thought about all the money she could make. But none of it would be hers. She would simply have to hand it right back to him.

She thought about the women down at the Lyndon Centre having coffee after the aerobics in their leotards. She thought about their badly proportioned bodies and how they always presented the worst parts to her saying: Can you do anything for that? While sitting on the stools their flabby thighs would be dripping over the edges. How often would they have to lift their legs or kick their legs out with the music to make the flab disappear? Then she thought of them all crowding around her with their pink breasts and their stripy stomachs, listening to her talk about Herbaslim. A crowd of women in leotards holding handbags. She would be working forever for Leo Stanley.

That evening, she discussed it with Derek as they got into bed.

'Do you think I should do it?' she asked, almost in a whisper.

'Of course you should, if you think there's money in it.'

She thought about his answer. He didn't seem to think about it very much because he was already gripping the flesh on the inside of her thigh, holding it up as if to be weighed.

Fog

The day she left, there was fog all over the estate. Thick fog. You could hardly see the houses on the opposite side of the road, or at the back beyond the small gardens. The place looked deserted too. And silent. You could have thrown a rock through a window, shattering glass everywhere, without anyone noticing. You could have stood naked at the front door. You could have slit your own throat. You could have disembowelled yourself on the lawn, nobody would have batted an eyelid. She must have waited for that morning with the fog.

Mike Spencer left the curtains closed for weeks. Nobody knew whether he was in or out. Nobody was aware of him coming home at night carrying cans of beer, more whiskey, take-aways, kebabs, fish and chips. Nobody saw him leave during the day. Nobody enquired.

He knew she wasn't coming back. He had tried everything. She said this time it was for good. Nothing he would do would ever persuade her to go back and live with him in that 'Jesus awful fucking depressing' estate again. Nothing. And nothing would ever get her to live with him, ever, anywhere again. It was over. 'Finito' was her final word on the phone before she slammed it down.

He considered his options. He could be realistic and forget her. He could track her down and confront her in public. Maybe he could find some way of making her jealous, making her think about the great times they had, when they were inseparable. He missed her, physically, consciously, affectionately, biologically... he could still feel her in the bedroom, hear her on the stairs; he could still see her laughing, throwing her head back. He needed her. He felt as empty as an empty pop song.

He sat in the kitchen with the smell of stale beer and vinegar hanging in the air, cleared a triangle of space for himself among the empty beer cans and opened the Golden Pages. A book for desperate people. The last resort of the lonely; the undecided. He moved randomly from back to front, absently reading out the ads. He thought of hiring a chainsaw, something to make a bit of noise with. He thought of calling a plumber, for company. Then he came to the Kissogram service. The ad had a small line drawing of a chambermaid, or a waitress in a small white apron, wearing fishnet stockings. The chambermaid was carrying a heart. A throbbing heart.

He picked up the phone and dialled the number. The girl who answered had a sweet voice; a carnal voice; a fellatio voice. Then he had an idea that she was a girl who ate crisps all day, a fat girl who was hired for her thin, luscious, shapely voice. He booked his request. She took the details; the address, the date, the exact time requested.

'It's for a friend. A colleague who has just got a big promotion; sales director. You know. We're having a small party. We want to play this trick on him.'

'I understand,' she said in a sweet, encouraging voice. Then she asked how he wanted to pay.

'Mastercard,' he said, slowly giving out the number first, then the expiry date.

The girl on the phone read everything back to him to make sure it was correct. He thanked her. He asked if she would make a note beside the address; it was the top flat, the very top. 'I'll make a note of that, sir,' she said. It made him feel older, more prosperous, more respectable.

He looked down at the Kissogram ad in the directory once more. The chambermaid's lips were swollen. He took a pen and began to distort her legs and her hips. He extended her décolletage.

What does the Kissogram girl do all day? Today she is having a driving lesson. She has to concentrate, keep looking in the mirror. She smells the scent of pine in the car and wonders if the driving instructor is immune to it. He is immune to her. He has no idea that she is a Kissogram girl at night. All this concentration makes her forget about it too. There are things you have to put out of your mind, parts of yourself, parts of your life. Memory management. She likes to think of herself as an out-of-work actress, just doing this Kissogram thing for a laugh, to improve the cash flow.

What does Mike Spencer do all day? He walks a lot. He's a compulsive pedestrian. Occasionally he will stop into a bar, but he prefers to be on the move. Walking is a cure for love. He pursues a strictly random course by which each turn is chosen only on immediate impulse at the end of the street. Right or left? This way he can pretend he is really going somewhere in his life. Whenever he stops walking, he begins to think, to revert; and inevitably he will remember the woman who has just left him: her eyes, her laugh, her lip marks left behind on teacups. Her legs.

The Kissogram girl likes the city best at night, just after the rain has stopped. The city stretches out before her with choice; with beads of rainwater. Her driver and escort is the

Gorilla, whose head is like a hood, flung back to reveal the real man underneath. All men are gorillas, she thinks. But she enjoys the protection of his company as an escort. She stretches out her legs in the car in order to pull up her fish-net stockings. She declines the invitation to go for a drink later on with the Gorilla, but tells him to ask her again. She might change her mind. She likes a working partner who doesn't parade his desires. Her escort is discreet. He's civilized.

He stops the car at the Huntsman's Lounge. The next contract. The Gorilla pulls his hood over his head and his voice becomes muffled. He gives an impressive growl.

'Here we go,' she says, extracting herself from her over-coat, checking herself in the mirror before skipping across to the entrance of the lounge in her high heels. The Gorilla opens the door for her and they walk towards a group of men standing at the bar. The Gorilla behind her arouses attention with a loud mechanical rattle.

Just short of the group, the Kissogram girl seeks out a corpulent man holding a pint in his hand, slowly turning around to face her.

'Are you Charles Grogan?' she asks firmly. The man nods and gives a contrived laugh.

'Yah bastards,' he shouts genially, turning to his friends. But he really is quite flattered, anxious to see what will happen next. The chambermaid's dress reveals most of her thighs. Enough to turn any man into an ape. He can't help looking down at her legs, particularly at the right thigh, which is demonstrably sloped forward and adorned with a white garter from which the Kissogram girl takes a thin handwritten scroll. She unrolls it with maximum ceremony, swinging her hips with absolute command over men. Everybody is watching, and listening. The barmen are smiling.

'Yah bastards!' repeated the man, this time silently, forming the words without sound.

The Kissogram girl began to read the rhyming lines from the scroll. Everyone laughed. Men ran their fingers along their ties with excitement. The barmen kept playing with glasses. Somebody whispered about her legs. Somebody else hidden from her view simulated standing copulation with thrusting hips and received an ugly stare from the Gorilla. The victim stood nervously smiling with his pint in his hand when the Kissogram girl finally replaced the scroll in her garter. With a dramatized gesture, she stepped forward, flung her arms around him and placed a noisy, smacking kiss on his face, leaving behind a large print of her lips on his cheek. His friends cheered in unison: Ooooooh. The Gorilla jumped and rattled.

That was it. The victim stood motionless, pinned back by the kiss, while the Kissogram girl marched out on the arm of her primitive escort, followed by the stares of men, wishing they could see more of her legs, and more of her swaying hips.

'Yah dirty bastards,' was all he could say, affectionately, to his friends, before beckoning the barman and ordering pints for all. There was no question of wiping his face or rubbing off the precious kiss.

'I'm starving,' the Kissogram girl said as soon as she got back into the car. She pulled her coat around her. The Gorilla threw back his face.

'We'll pick up a kebab before the next call. We have lots of time,' he said.

'Jesus no. I couldn't eat a kebab. I'd smell a mile.'

'Burger, chips?' he suggested.

At a small takeaway, a man in an advanced state of drunken torpor stared at the menu. He couldn't believe his eyes. After much concentration, he ordered chips. What else? He had to hold on to the counter for support. At one of the tables there was a woman eating a kebab, her face tilted.

When the Gorilla walked in, the drunk at the counter began to stare at the furry arms. He staggered backwards and read the sign on the Gorilla's back. Kiss-O-Gram. The words made him dizzy, sending him back to hold on to the counter, shaking the words from his head.

The Kissogram girl came in, whispered to the Gorilla and sat down close to the door, wrapped in her coat. The drunk was given his chips. He turned and leaned against the counter so that he could concentrate on picking out a single chip and balancing it into his mouth. His eyes fell on the Kissogram girl with unexpected clarity.

'Ah me darlin',' he said, stumbling forward to embrace her, offering her chips. She shook her head and pushed him away, brutally.

'Piss off,' she said.

The man staggered back. A number of chips fell to the floor. He would have continued going backwards if he hadn't been stopped by the counter.

'You're no fuckin' lady . . .' he said. His male pride was among the chips on the floor. He might have been more effective had he not been so drunk. The Kissogram girl circumvented the mess and walked out. The Gorilla followed her carrying two bags of food, growling as he passed. The drunk stared after them, bewildered, not knowing that he was spilling the remaining chips, one by one.

The Kissogram girl eats without allowing food to touch her lips. She lives for her lips. Afterwards, she applies a new layer of lipstick, forming an O with her mouth. She practised a kiss on the window of the car, half intended for a pedestrian, a man standing on the pavement. She laughs at

68

the wasted kiss. She applies new lipstick. She is ready for the next assignment.

They stopped outside a house on Northumberland Road. The Gorilla checked the address. She placed a new scroll in her garter and stepped out on to the pavement. The pavement was still sticky from the rain. They found the right door. They were let in by an intercom system and switched on a timed lightswitch on the stairs. They climbed the stairs and found the top-floor flat where the door had been left slightly ajar. Music emerged; the sound of a party. The Kissogram girl paused to catch her breath. The light on the landing went out. Ready. She adjusted her scroll and then pushed the door open, striding in with the rattling, guffawing ape behind her.

But there was no party. There was only one man sitting in an armchair reaching over to switch off the music. The Gorilla stopped rattling. They were in silence. Had they got the wrong address? She felt as though she had made a big mistake and was ready to apologize until she suddenly recognized the man in the chair.

'Jesus, Michael. Why are you doing this to me? How did you get here? Who told you?' She looked puzzled. Angry.

Mike Spencer smiled. 'It's the only way I can get to talk to you. You ignore me. You never answer the phone. I need to talk to you.'

'I told you, I don't want to discuss it. Why don't you leave me alone? It's over. Can't you get that into your thick skull?'

The Gorilla behind her clapped back his hood and looked even more fierce underneath; annoyed for her sake, ready to defend his Kissogram girl. She folded her arms in hostility.

The Gorilla spoke out. 'Listen mate. Why don't you lay off?'

Mike Spencer ignored him and asked her to sit down.

'Look Mike, I'm finished with you. This is a really low, dirty trick. You'll never get me that way. Now leave me alone, will you?'

She turned to go but crashed into the Gorilla. It was all very awkward. You can never get away cleanly.

'Wait, Claire,' Mike shouted.

'No.'

'You owe me something. Wait. I paid for a Kissogram. You're obliged to give me that at least.'

She is forced to turn around again. Professional ethics.

'Look Michael,' she said, softening a little. 'There is nothing for us to talk about any more. I know how you feel, but there is nothing I can do. It's over. I want to be left alone.'

'Just five minutes . . .' he pleaded.

The Kissogram girl turned around to the Gorilla and asked him to wait for her in the car. She would sort this out herself and join him in five minutes. The Gorilla was reluctant to leave her with this unstable creature, her past lover. But she persuaded him to leave. She wouldn't be long. She could handle it.

'Yeh, get lost, you big fucking gorilla,' Mike shouted after him. Both men exchanged a ferocious stare. She avoided anything worse by closing the door.

She sat down, aware that she was showing far too much of her legs. She crossed them. She stared at him and tried to remain furious. Underneath, perhaps she was beginning to yield, tacitly beginning to admire his cunning determination; the elaborate pretence which brought her here.

'You know it kills me to see you like this,' he said. 'Selling your kisses to strangers.'

She shrugged. Her bosom rippled. She had an outrageous cleavage, with a false beauty spot. She refused to explain anything.

'Look at me, Claire,' he pleaded. 'Look at me . . . look into my eyes. Can't you see what you're doing?'

She stood up and turned her back on him. It was the only way she could keep herself from regressing, from falling back into his love. He noticed the lines imprinted on her legs by the chair. He noticed her shaking. She was crying. The Kissogram girl was crying.

He could have gone over to her and placed his hands on her shoulders. He could have kissed her neck and said: 'Claire, don't cry, please.' He could have turned the lights down. Offered her a drink. Kissed her eyes. He might have said: 'Claire, do you remember the day you saw me off on the train in London?' He could have tickled her. He might have put his arm around her waist and embraced her from behind. He could have allowed his hand to run upwards along the inside of her thighs, along the fishnet stockings. He could have lifted her chambermaid's uniform and whispered: 'Claire, come on, let's go to bed.' He might have felt pity, or despair, or anger. He could have raised his voice and said: 'Why do we always have to go through this pretence?' He could have attacked her. He could have stabbed her in the back. Plunged a blade straight between her ribs. He could have killed her quickly.

She was unable to turn around and face him. Unable to stop herself crying. Eventually he got up and moved towards her. She jumped when he touched her, but then allowed herself to be drawn back. She sat down in the armchair, avoiding his gaze.

'Will I tell the Gorilla to go home?' He whispered.

She didn't answer. She had acceded. He left her there and quietly walked out. Halfway down the stairs, the lights went out and he had to grope along the wall for the switch. He opened the front door and walked down the path and through the gate where he saw the Gorilla sitting in the car. He saw the wasted kiss on the car window, and the Gorilla's perfidious stare. He could have leaned into the car and told the Gorilla he might as well go home, she was staying. Instead, he ignored the car and went straight across the road, walking away all the time. Before he got to the end of the street, he turned around to see the Gorilla running from the car into the house.

In Dublin Where the Palm Trees Grow

Front door open wide for Alberta sunshine along a Dublin hallway. No sound. Air outside almost as passive as the inside of the house which seems like the carriage of a train stopped in the middle of a prairie. Passengers look to each other for explanations, stretch their legs, adjust their clothes, look at the time and brush crumbs from the seating with spooned hands. Scratch their heads, avoid each other, make the beds and open the windows to look down at the children already playing outside in the bushes. Sound of hissing comes from the kitchen where the windows have steamed up. Sound of a mouth organ or something from the next carriage. Local flies come in to investigate this house pushed on to their land. Two local children appear black against the sunlight in the doorway to see if lunch is ready.

And that piano has always been there in the hallway. No place for it anywhere else. Can't be sold or repaired. The children often bash out a few warped notes on their way in or out, gratuitously. Not good enough for them to learn on. And at night on the way home from the pub, children asleep, babysitter gone home, they used to drag a chair into the hallway. Sometimes even lighting candles in the brass holders. Sometimes, sitting on his knee, they would sing 'The Moon Stood Still', quietly at first and then as loud as they could go. Sometimes making her hands play the warped chords by holding on to her white wrists till they hurt. Sometimes dancing while they sang, while one of his hands still beat out the lazy chord. Sometimes falling hard against the piano. And when the song was over, somebody would say 'This is stupid', and they would start all over again or go to bed. The chair would be still there in the morning to remind them. Perhaps a scarf or a jacket or one of her shoes still lying around in the hallway as well.

But that was before the guy moved in upstairs. Always the smell of curry up there now. Now the babies have turned into boys. Now it's their turn to bash the piano with mocking daytime notes, meant only for the night. And the sound of that mouth organ or whatever from next door. Always seem to be dancing in there during the day.

Man next door on the other side is worse. He cut down his side of the hedge, exposing a wall of branches. Exposing neighbours to each other, exposing gaps in the dark green hedge which screens the front garden of wild bushes and prairie grass from all the other gardens and houses on the street. And the single palm which they always want their father to climb, always shivering in the Dublin rain, always so dusty in the midday sun. They shoot each other under the palm and come in to lunch fighting. Somebody refused to die.

She deals out the food. Chicken and mashed potatoes. They sit around the table without a word until she's finished. Nobody is allowed to speak until they begin. They all begin at the same time, each person looking at his own plate to see what they got. Each looking around to see that nobody got more. Each chewing quietly to themselves.

Tommy looks up at his father.

'Daddy, isn't it true that I was born in Montreal?' His father gives a nod of acknowledgement without taking his eyes off his own plate. Tommy turns to his brother. 'See, I told you.'

74

The younger boy looks to his mother to restore equality. She winks at him and looks at his father.

'You were born right here in Dublin, same as your dad. And you've got your dad's forehead too.'

Who was that meant for? He looks up from his plate to see if she meant anything. But there's nothing telling in her eyes. She looks at the boys and tells them to eat – the pair of you. Then he looks at the youngest.

'We ran out of cities by the time we got to you,' he says, glancing back at her again. The boys don't understand. It was meant for her.

'You would have been born in Vancouver but your mummy wanted to come back to Dublin instead.'

Something telling in her eyes now.

'Come on Michael, let them eat now,' she says openly. Without a further word, she taps her fork on the edge of each of their plates. The boys take this up and tap each other's plates. Everybody taps everyone else's plate and she is forced to disclose her amusement with a short smile, enough to laugh and still maintain order. Nothing that would give her away.

The boys continue to argue. The front door is still open to the occasional fly which leaves again after a frenzied indoor flight, and for the Alberta sun which almost reaches the base of the piano. She stirs the pot and asks if anyone wants more. Tommy wonders if he's a Canadian.

'You were born two days after we got married,' his father says.

The game is up. She puts down her knife and fork noisily. As if she has seen something disgusting on her plate. She looks at him with a sickly expression on her face, gets up from the table and walks out. He doesn't follow. He thinks it's a bluff.

*

Man from upstairs appears in the kitchen doorway without warning, like an official. He should ring the doorbell or knock at least. It's so sudden, he might have been standing there for ages. Not even a cough. What can you do but smile and fumble with the dishcloth. She's much firmer. She would have told him to get out and knock.

Wants to know if he can have some help to carry a table upstairs. Smell of garlic would choke you. The boys want to help too and follow the table on its way up the stairs.

At the same time, she emerges again from the bedroom, closing the bedroom door behind her. The bedroom door has a Yale lock, like any hall door on to the street. On her way back into the kitchen, she passes below the point where the table is sloped on the stairs, without looking up, as if it were indecent.

The man at the Montreal registry office was so sympathetic. Would nearly have paid for the organ services out of his own pocket, had they even half wanted it. Seemed personally shocked at their reaction. 'We don't need the organ, do we?' they said, looking at each other. They wanted no flowers either. What use had they for exhibition when she moved so heavily pregnant beside him?

'You can stop eating off the floor now,' he says to the man upstairs when they finally get the table into position. The remark doesn't go down well. The man upstairs is thin and serious, says he works in a restaurant in town. Can you trust a man like that who says thank you three times in a row? The boys have come all the way up to investigate new territory. They look down through the top windows and see a dog intrude into their garden so they run down the stairs again growling. The man upstairs seems nervous. Conversation is superficial, at arm's length. Says he likes Pink

Floyd records. That says it all. He says thank you again. Anytime. Thanks a lot. Anytime. Keep away. Anytime. Thank you.

The only witness at their wedding was the Moroccan barman, Mustafa. Stocky, with hair like black lambswool. They were obliged to bring someone to sign the papers. 'Kill the papers,' he said. It was Mustafa's word for everything. 'Kill the glasses' meant wash the glasses. 'Kill the windows.' 'Kill the ashtrays.' On the day of the wedding, the three of them sat on meretricious red velvet seats, surrounded by dark wood, half listening to the registrar's leatherbound words. The registrar was doing his best, only to become visibly embarrassed when he took it for granted that there was a ring. Mustafa rushed back to work after the ceremony, shook hands and told them to come to the bar later to kill some beers. They had to wait for the papers to be sealed. On the way down the steps outside, an eager photographer was ready to take the shots, until he realized her state with a knowing smile.

She looks out through the kitchen window and sees, beyond the granite back garden wall, the outstretched hands of somebody next door taking down the washing from the line. The arms seem to have no body. They reach up like somebody sinking in a swamp. Every time a garment is released, the washing line bounces back up again and the arms slip further down.

On a train, the only safe place to look is out through the windows.

Nothing moves much out there in the back. The garden has been reclaimed by undergrowth. A long time ago, somebody must have tried to cultivate that soil and then abandoned it again. Later on, there will be midges hovering in the air. The land outside will look parched like a dried-up lake.

Afterwards, they walked back along a different route away from the registry office. As if they had to forget where they came from, or dodge pursuit. But they moved so slowly, she was so close to the birth, that they had time to memorize each step as they passed. Then came the car park. And after the car park came the railings with the blue creeper reaching to the pavement. Everything went by so slowly, relatively, like distant trees seen from a train. The shops. The parking meters.

When they came to a café, it was time for her to sit down again. He bought cheesecake and coffee, just to celebrate, he said in spite of himself. But she never finished the cake. Her heartburn. In the middle of it, she stood up without a word and went to the washroom. He was expecting it to begin any moment, not knowing what to expect, half expecting her to emerge holding a baby. The whole city of Montreal had become a waiting room.

On the way out of the café, they passed more trays with cakes and she said they always looked better behind glass. And he could only see her gravid reflection in the glass. And she moved on so slowly, it made him want to run. As if she had eaten a huge pink cake. Occasionally, she stalled on the pavement. Almost pulling him back. They realized for the first time what it was like to be old. The more they moved on, the more they seemed to stand still.

It was to be the most insignificant day of their lives. They didn't care for weddings. A marriage certificate bore no relevance to them. But they moved too slowly to escape. The day they most eagerly sought to forget could only have become the day they would always remember most. She even remembers Mustafa's shirt with its buttoned-down collar. And the registrar's cufflinks.

A day to forget. A day to be played down. That's how they wanted it at the time. So she believed. So she believed he believed. Because they talked mostly with their eyes then.

The front door is still open, though the sun has moved away from the piano. Outside, somebody has begun to cut a lawn with the usual sound. Later, the air will be full of midges and the smell of cut grass.

He used to await her time like a birthday every month. Something to celebrate almost. He could answer any question about her. What colour underwear she wore. What skin cream she used. Now, it has all become more vague. He only realizes when she mentions it or when he sees the box of tampons on her dressing table. Only realizes when she asks – 'What day is today?' – that she is taking the pill again and throwing the packet back into the drawer beside the bed. Only realizes when he hears her breathing slowed down that she sometimes falls asleep before him. On his way down the stairs from the flat upstairs, he is surprised to find himself thinking about her. Surprised to remember that it was more than a week ago that she had brought out the tampon box. She still tells him every time.

'Because I don't want the whole world to know where and how I got married,' she says angrily when they meet again in the breakfast room. 'It's not fair. It's my information.'

She becomes silent again. They are both sitting across the table from each other, alone. She's still keeping to herself. But there's more anger there now. Something telling in her eyes.

He doesn't reply. He has nothing to say. And because he

says nothing, it seems as though he has a lot to say.

'It's not fair, Michael. Maybe you don't realize that some of these things are personal. Next thing you'll be telling them where they were conceived. You might as well go out into the street and tell everybody.'

Instead of agreeing with her, he contrives some vague argument about her being secretive. Deceiving herself. He notices the effort with which she says these things. She seems softer, now that she has said it all.

'I believe in being totally honest,' he says. 'I'm not hiding anything.'

He knows what he says is untrue. He knows it provokes her. Calls her bluff. Because she looks straight up at him, unable to hold down her tears.

'You shit, Michael. You know we agreed on that. You agreed not to tell anyone, ever.'

He looks away through the window. Nothing moves much out there. Nobody ever goes into the back garden. He sees a fence pole which has begun to slant over the path. Somebody must have leaned on it sometime.

That night, on their way back from the pub, they recognized their house by the palm tree outside. The breeze has caught the leatherette leaves, flat green tails with ragged ends, making them flap. The breeze has come in from the coast, past the yachts, past the harbour lights and past the palm trees. Past sun umbrellas growing out of the centre of round outdoor tables outside the hotel. Past flapping canopies outside shops. The breeze must have started up somewhere in the Pacific. Tonga.

He opens the door and lets her walk into the house before him. He shuts the door quietly. She goes straight to the bedroom and unlocks the door, like a house within a house. He stops by the piano and plays a few idle notes, just the start of a song, no more. But the sound seems so warped, as if a strong wind had followed them in through the hall door and carried off the notes.

As he follows her into the bedroom, he sees that she is already half undressed. He is surprised to see that she is wearing shiny, silk-like underwear. He has never seen them before. But he doesn't let on that he has noticed and she doesn't let on that she wants him to notice. She says nothing, without letting on that she's said nothing. He goes to the dressing table and takes his watch off. He begins to work on the knot of his tie. He hasn't said anything and doesn't let on he's in the bedroom yet. In the mirror, he sees her standing on the far side of the bed. He has noticed that her hands meet between her legs and that she covers the silk-like material with a slow, mechanical movement. Her hair has fallen over her eyes, letting on that there is nobody in the room but herself. He can observe her in the mirror without letting on that he's watching or that he's stopped undoing his tie.

'What day is today?'

As he falls asleep, he is held back by the feeling that the whole house is moving and that the front door has been left open.

'Did you kill the front door?' she asks.

'I sang the door through the palm trees . . . stopped . . . on your arm . . .'

In the morning, she looks out through the bedroom window and sees that they are still in the same place. The fence leaning out over the path. The weeds. The brown, dried-up Christmas tree, fallen on its side, almost submerged in the rugged grass. And the circular, black, charred patch where somebody had once lit a fire. A long time ago. Drifters.

The Compound Assembly of E. Richter

Frank Murray woke up to the sound of hammering. He half hoped that the noise would abate or that sleep would win back its grip. But the window was open and the noise persisted. It quickly distinguished itself from any other sound as that of scaffolding. The enclosed courtyard amplified it. Even though Frank was on the fourth floor it seemed as if they were erecting scaffolding right outside his window. In Germany, nobody sleeps during the day. Even those who work at night lie in bed at their own peril in the morning.

He tried to shut the window without getting up. From his bed, or his mattress on the floor, he reached up and pushed on the frame with his fingers. He caught sight of the workmen in grey-and-blue overalls. They were further away than he thought. They were working on the opposite face of the courtyard. It wasn't enough to close out the noise and he had to reach further to lock the handle. In doing this, his body became uncovered. The duvet only covered half his thighs, breaking the nocturnal spell of warmth. His naked body, like sensitive photographic paper, had been exposed to daylight. He locked the window and drew himself back under the duvet. It turned steel into rubber.

He couldn't sleep again. He coiled his knees up and held his shoulders with his hands. The sound still penetrated the window. He stretched his legs and found both the bed and duvet were too short. It was useless. He resolved to get up.

Frank rehearsed the next ten minutes of the day in his mind. Going to the shop next door to buy some rolls and apricot jam. Opening the door of the apartment. Descending the stairs. Seeing the rows of mailboxes which faced him on the way down, each with its metal door and small glass window through which he might see a letter from home but which more often turned out to be circulars and postal advertising which he then regularly stuck into somebody else's letter box. Seeing that many of the metal doors had been prised open by owners who'd lost their keys. Checking with his longest fingers to make sure there wasn't a letter from home which, whenever one did arrive, he kept unopened in his pocket for hours, sometimes even till evening when he would find a secluded pub where he could read and slowly get drunk with his letter. Cautiously removing his fingers from under the sharp metal door. Emerging out into the courtyard where the climate is thick with work, shouts, commands, hammering and where German workers belittle each other with diligence. Seeing how far they had got with the scaffolding. Walking through the outer door into the street. Lifting one jar of apricot jam but then replacing it again in preference for another brand.

On his way back from the shop carrying a white plastic bag, Frank saw a woman's back beside the mailboxes. She had just locked her metal door and begun to turn around. He had seen her before in the same position. She was always locking her letter box. The stairs were ahead of him. The rise between the third and fourth step bore a warning. '*Vorsicht!*' On Tuesdays, the stairs are freshly polished. On Tuesdays, the climate indoors is clean but highly slippery.

With one foot already flung into the first part of his ascent, Frank pronounced the obliged greeting clearly. '*Guten Morgen!*' It was addressed at the woman's back and seemed to rebound off her shoulders. It came back abbreviated. '*Morgen!*'

His feet had already passed the warning sign, entering the second phase of ascent, taking steps in doubles. The plastic bag with apricot jam and rolls swung forward in counterbalance. His left foot had just pushed off the step when she addressed him again from below.

'*Sind Sie der Herr der so schön die Flöte spielt?*' He stopped and his left foot recanted. He turned and made a quick translation: Are you the gentleman who so lovely the flute plays? He brought back the other foot to the step below and fumbled an answer. *Ja!* It was always a pleasure to hear comments about his music. It was always a compliment to be asked about his nationality. It was good to be Irish in Germany. As long as they didn't want to know about Northern Ireland or the *EEh-Er-Ah* (IRA). As long as they stuck to music or the Cliffs of Moher or smoked salmon or Heinrich Böll or donkeys or red hair and freckles and the agrarian state.

Frank smiled over the banister at her and nodded to secure his answer. He welcomed any compliment. But she didn't smile back at him. She had clutched her keys to her chest and looked straight up at him. He waited for a moment to see if the question of nationality would arise. But there was something wrong with her expression. It held more accusation than admiration.

'*Wenn ich diesen Lärm weiter höre, kommt die Polizei.*' The last word was enough. If she heard any more of this noise, she would call the police. The sudden conversion of an admirer into an enemy had left him completely stunned and awkwardly poised on the stairs. His feet, drawn by compliment, were still subconsciously coming back down. Frank said nothing.

'*Sie wohnen bei Evelyn Richter, nicht wahr?*' He wasn't quite sure whether this was meant to confirm that he was living with Evelyn Richter or staying with Evelyn Richter. There was a big difference. Evelyn Richter was the name on his mailbox. That much was right. He was living in her apartment, but in his own separate room. Werner, Evelyn's boyfriend, was living with her.

Frank wasn't about to start explaining anything to the woman with the keys to her chest who had led him into a trap. The glare of her questions over the banisters had registered an insult with him and he turned to continue his climb with redoubled speed.

When Evelyn heard about the incident, she created too much of a fuss. At teatime that evening she became very excited.

'*Unglaublich!* It is unbelievable,' she said. She was laying the table at the time. She used wooden boards instead of plates. Her cutlery matched. She placed another board with an assortment of ham, sausage and cheese on the table. She had also chopped some radishes which looked like white coins with red rims. *Ten-pfennig* pieces.

'I will go to this woman and tell her she has nothing to say. She has not the right to say this to you. It is unbelievable.'

Evelyn shook her head. She had straight sandy hair which normally hung to one side. Whenever she looked at someone, she had the habit of slanting her head sideways.

'Wait! I will tell this to Werner when he comes. This woman will hear something from us.'

Frank rarely saw Evelyn's eyes because she wore tinted brown glasses. He was leaning against the radiator with his arms folded. She told him to sit down and placed the earthenware teapot on a candle-lit warmer. Frank asked where Werner was and heard he was visiting his mother. There was a small two-pronged fork lying along the board with the ham. It often looked so decorative that Frank didn't think he should disturb it. He lifted the fork and speared a slice of smoked ham, separating it from the next layer. Evelyn asked him to describe the woman.

'*Ach* . . . this is Frau Klempner. We know this woman. She is always looking and talking to the *Hausmeister*.' Evelyn made a duck's beak with her hand to describe.

'Do you know this word, "*plappern*"?'

'It sounds very much like the word prattle in English,' Frank explained, thinking of yet another word, 'babble'. Again, there was a white sheen across Evelyn's glasses. Her mime often explained things much better than her words.

Frank would have ignored the incident or passed it off as one more example of German life to be handed on as a gift or a passing joke to some other fellow musician travelling in Germany. His instinct told him to keep playing his pipes and whistles even louder in spite of this Frau Klempner. But Evelyn made more of it. She treated him as a helpless musician affronted by a typically tyrannical German woman. All art and music had been assaulted by this philistine, Frau Klempner. For Frank, even though it was comforting to be defended by a young woman, the incident was amusing. For Evelyn, it was an attack on freedom. It even infringed her own privacy.

'I don't ask her to close her windows when she's cooking and the stink of onions is everywhere in the courtyard.'

Werner was far more rational. He laughed and said Frau Klempner should be ignored. She had no authority. He seemed tired and sat back in the sofa with his beer. He dismissed the whole thing with a wave of his hand which looked as though he was declining the offer of cake.

'This old one. She has nothing to say.'

Evelyn sat down facing Werner with her knees on the sofa. Her shoes had dropped to the floor. Werner had a layer of froth on his moustache. Evelyn reached over and lifted some of the froth clinging to her finger and put it in her own mouth. Werner then placed his own finger across his moustache and caught the remaining froth with his lower lip.

Three sides of the wide courtyard are covered with windows. The other is a wall hung with scaffolding. Some of the walls between the windows are peeling. Some of the windows have a white sheet across them. The workmen have gone home leaving behind an aftersound of planks and shouts.

Frank saw Evelyn coming across the courtyard in a long coat. He was on his way out while she was coming in. She carried a leather bag which was meant more for documents than for personal things. She looked different. It was the first time he had seen her wearing that coat. It was the first time he had seen her at a distance, walking towards him. She seemed smaller. The new perspective of the open courtyard with its windows and scaffolding made her look compact. He saw her as somebody he didn't know.

The furniture in her apartment makes Evelyn Richter stand out. The immured dimensions of her apartment give an illusion of size. Tables, chairs, sofa, the eighteen-inch television set alter her shape. The height of the pictures hung in her apartment make her seem more friendly. The poster in the kitchen of the Folies Bergère. The shoes beside the sofa make her younger, more like a child. In the courtyard, she looks smaller, fuller, more official and unknown.

She looks like part of the underground throngs. An individual observed on a crowded train. An unknown person with an imagined unlimited biography. A person in a long beige coat carrying a leather bag. A rather official-looking bag. A person without gender on the way home from work. A person who buys a monthly ticket. A young woman with a public smile for the ticket vendor.

She looks like a person whose mother might own a dachshund or a red setter. A person who has just bought some cheese or unsalted butter at the cheese shop. Who paused briefly before putting her U-bahn ticket into her bag. Who thought she was being stared at by an elderly man on the U-bahn. Who avoids making eye contact on the underground trains. Whose view of two children is blocked by someone standing in front of her on the U-bahn. Who glances at the headlines of the evening paper in someone else's hands and who looks away again because it's unmannerly and would also form an association with the man sitting down with his evening paper. Who holds on firmly to the vertical bar on the U-bahn whenever she can't get a seat. Who looks at the familiar, numberless clock on her way out of the U-bahn station. Who held her bag against the counter of the cheese shop with her knee while she took out her purse. Who heard the combined surge of traffic behind her after she had crossed the road. Who had hoped that the green man would stay green a little longer.

A person who has just placed a packet of Danish cheese along with a packet of unsalted butter into a rather official-looking bag. Who passes the wine shop without hesitation. Passes the Eros centre without noticing it. Who has never even been inside a sex shop. Passes a Turkish woman in the street with her child and wonders how a Turkish woman can wear so many layers of clothes, even in spring. Who thinks Turkish children look pretty. Feels a slight dampness under her arms. Thought Danish cheese would be nice for tea. Never eats garlic. Who has never been to South America but would love to go. Who has never been to Ireland but who knows somebody from Ireland. Who has no wish to go to Turkey ever because there are so many Turkish people living in Berlin. Never speaks about school and never associates with any of her old classmates. Who hates a man called Dieter Opp and who hopes she will never see him again. Who is not too keen on her parents coming to visit her in Berlin.

For whom the conglomerate smell of cheeses at the cheese shop becomes too much after a few minutes. Who emerges from the cheese shop and glances right and left looking for inspiration before continuing her journey home. Who loves Greek food and Greek music. Finds Irish music haunting and medieval. Cannot stand Eastern music. Who used to like South American music but who has gone off it somewhat lately. Finds Irish people more European than a lot of Italians. Finds unsalted butter much more pleasant than the salted ones. Finds it incomprehensible that her brother would join the army, particularly after what happened to their father during the war. Whose father refuses to speak about the war. Who writes a letter to her brother asking him not to join the army but receives no answer from him.

Has a general phobia about posting letters which causes a moment of fear and irreversible helplessness once the letter disappears. Once had an older man from Charlottenburg for a boyfriend but put an end to it because he began to remind her too much of her father. Who still tends to compare all boyfriends with her father. Who can't help thinking about her own letter at the bottom of the yellow postbox. Who always insists on discussing all her previous affairs and relationships with any new boyfriend and expects them to do the same. Who tends to bite with abject ferocity at that moment when approaching rapture with her lover. Who was warned many times by one man never again to use her teeth but forgets herself sometimes, causing him once to walk out in the middle of the night saying he would never be back, but did return a week later and was no longer welcome. Though he managed to sleep with her once more, she made sure she didn't bite him on that final turn. Who has a steady relationship which has gone on for the past few years with one man. Who is in no rush to have a baby. Who has orgasms. Who does not bite her current boyfriend.

Is in possession of a sad feature in her eyes which illuminates a paternal longing in all men. Whose strange blend of sadness and comical appearance is noticed on the U-bahn. Whose skin attracts mosquitoes. Whose eyes are normally hidden by her lightly tinted glasses. Who has a slight tendency to put on weight around the thighs and who suppresses this with regular swimming followed by saunas. Whose hand firmly clutches the bar on the U-bahn between the grip of an older man and that of a younger man. Who doesn't notice the collection of knuckles along the bar. Who is observed in detail by the younger man looking at her knuckles and following her wrist along the sleeve to trace its owner. Whose head is turned away from the young man on the U-bahn who has been studying her arm, her hair and her knuckles and contemplated pressing on one of her knuckles to make her turn around so that he could see if the face matched what the hair and knuckles promised. Whose face with its sad look does belong to the knuckles along the vertical bar.

Who received an expensive camera once from her current partner in the early days of their relationship and only shot two rolls of colour film on their first holiday after which she abandoned it. Who would very dearly like to gain possession of a particular photograph which was taken years ago on a time release which shows her smiling and clutching a bottle of champagne while being embraced from behind by

Dieter Opp with his hand inside her pink knickers and his chin resting on her left shoulder glancing downwards at her naked breasts. Who is known in the cheese shop. Who carries a bag which does not look like it contains anything such as Danish cheese or unsalted butter. Of whom it is often difficult to tell whether she's looking straight ahead or downwards. Who knows what time it is. Whose hand holds the handle of her bag. Who pushes the heavy front door of the house with her shoulder. Who wears a knee-length coat. Whose arms are inside the coat. Whose hair touches the collar of the coat. Whose chin is round. Whose feet touch the ground. Who has eyes. Who can speak. Breathes, hears, sees in front of her. Is an inhabitant of Berlin.

The windows on all three sides look out on to the courtyard. The tenants can all see out on to their courtyard which has a cluster of olive trees along with some flower-boxes as its central feature. It is difficult to tell when people are actually looking out on to their courtyard. Some windows are left open. The tenants are discouraged from hanging out washing through the windows.

Evelyn and Frank meet in the courtyard some ten metres away from the centre. They stop and talk for a moment. The courtyard with all its windows forces them to meet as strangers or people who just know each other vaguely. Frank is in a rush and has a box containing his instruments under his arm. With a clenched fist he tries to indicate running or lateness or hurry. Evelyn has stopped and is holding her bag with both hands. Frank tries to leave on a humorous note.

'What have you done to Frau Klempner? I haven't seen her in weeks. Have you done away with her?'

Evelyn smiles and shakes her head.

'Nothing! I leave her alone.' Evelyn has transferred her bag to the left hand.

*

The phone rang in the room, suspending his playing in mid-reel. There did follow just two more notes but they had already lost power. The instrument had been winded. The drones lost their momentum and expired. Even the invisible beat was overpowered by the new beat of the phone.

He placed his hand, holding the chanter, under the drones and walked over to the phone in a stoop. Placing one thigh and buttock on the armrest of the sofa, he cradled the pipes in his lap with his arm. The other leg, bound around the thigh with a leather piece like an eyepatch, was poised for balance, knee bent, ready to raise him up again. The green velvet bag with its meretricious tassels exhaled with a final sigh of unmusical breath. He crouched over the table and picked up the white receiver.

'Bei Richter,' he answered. It was Werner. He spoke in a calm, unhurried English. It was unusual to talk to Werner on the phone and Frank had to visualize his moustache before he could speak. He wondered if Werner had left something behind. But Werner was very conversational. Frank explained that he was keeping the evil spirit of Frau Klempner away with the sound of his uillean pipes.

'You have no concert tonight?' Werner asked. It amused Frank that all performances, even though most of his took place in small pubs, were referred to as concerts. He had taught Evelyn to call them 'gigs'.

'No, there's nothing on tonight. No concert.'

'Frank . . . if you have no plans tonight, we could meet us somewhere. I have something to discuss with you. Can we meet us in the restaurant Zum Römer? You know this one?'

Frank agreed and asked what they were going to discuss.

'We will talk about this at dinner, Zum Römer. Can we say eight o'clock?'

Frank closed his eyes and began to play again but he couldn't regain the drive of the music. He couldn't concentrate. It wasn't the first time Werner had formally announced that he was going to discuss something. Usually it was quite straightforward. The first thing was the matter of phone calls. Werner had asked him instead of leaving money beside the phone, to record them all in a booklet beside the phone which they could add up at the end of the month. Then there was the matter of a token rent for the room. Then there was the business of the cheese. This had been split into two issues. The fact that it was unfair to take the last piece of cheese without replacing it with more. Cheese was there to be eaten but only on condition that successors were provided for as well. The other issue concerned the way the cheese was cut, which was also with successors in mind. Cheese should not be approached from all sides at once and should never be cut between knife and thumb. They had many discussions which often spilled over into broader issues, preoccupied mainly with the difference between Germany and Ireland. Only once had the discussion gone too far when Frank had said: 'The only thing wrong with Germany is that it's not surrounded by water.' All other occasions had been more than friendly and disciplined.

When Frank arrived at the restaurant, Werner and Evelyn were already sitting at a table. He was surprised to see Evelyn there. He was also surprised to see that the Römer was otherwise empty. His memory of the Römer was that of a crowded restaurant. It was early. Frank made his way over to them as directly as possible. At one stage, he was forced to walk sideways between two chairs but keeping his destination in sight. He could have carried on along the wall behind Evelyn and Werner which showed the blanched sunlit steps leading down into the warm olive-lined streetscape of southern Italy. Werner shook hands.

'I have ordered a pizza for myself. You should have one too and a nice beer.' The waiter, having stalked Frank's diagonal progress across the restaurant, timed the moment with the sliding menu. At the same time, Evelyn raised her glass of red wine to her lips. Things were unusually formal. A decision was made and the waiter left, coming back moments later with a beer for Frank.

'The pizza here is the best in all Berlin,' Werner said. 'Nearly as good as in Italy.'

'Well, I've never been to Italy so I couldn't comment.'

'Ah, you must go! Evelyn and I, we have been in Italy three times since we met. It is very expensive but we like it very much.' Frank's eyes travelled from Werner to Evelyn and then on to the beer in front of him and in another circle back to Werner and then on to Evelyn again who was nodding in agreement.

'Of course. Italy is the best country for holidays,' she said.

Werner's pizza arrived followed shortly by Frank's pizza. The waiter had brought an extra plate for Evelyn who said she could only manage a small corner. As Werner began to cut a triangular slice, she repeated; not so much, not so much. Frank suggested it might be easier to cut a pizza with a pair of scissors. They laughed. It allowed Frank to slow down the circle which his eyes made around the table from Werner over to Evelyn and down to his own beer and on to Werner's pizza and Werner himself and back to Evelyn who was sitting up with her back straight, looking down at the geometric slice on the plate in front of her. Frank's own pizza gave him something to concentrate on. Werner's moustache appeared to be damp and curled into his mouth at one point. Evelyn cut a small triangle from the big triangle and raised it to her mouth on a fork.

It doesn't take long to eat a pizza. The only things left on Frank's plate are two olive stones. On Werner's, the stems of three chilli peppers. Behind Evelyn, on the wall, there is a pillar beyond which there is a woman bearing an urn on her way down to a hot plaza. Frank's beer is half full. Werner leans back in his chair and dusts off any possible crumbs from his trousers with his hand.

'Frank . . . I think you are waiting for me to discuss this with you now. It is something very important to me and to Evelyn also. For two weeks now, I have been thinking. In the beginning I thought it was only in my mind, but now I think I am right. I think Evelyn is falling in love with you.'

With thumb and forefinger, Werner parts his moustache to each side. Frank looks at Evelyn who has her elbows on the table. Her hair has partly fallen over her face. He looks at the ashtray on the table and then back to Werner.

'I have spoken to Evelyn about this. It is true. She has also agreed that something is happening to her. Frank . . . I don't want to make an accusation against you. I am not angry with you. But I think I must talk to you about this openly.'

Werner continues to explain. It has caught Frank like a compliment which he cannot instinctively deny. He could say nothing.

'I think about this every day now. All the time I think it is going to end with me and Evelyn. I think she will be in love with you very soon. I cannot stop it and I must talk to you before this happens.'

Evelyn has said nothing either. It looks almost as if she is incapable of acting involuntarily. Unharnessed. Why could she not just speak for herself? Frank's first impulse was to turn to Evelyn and ask her directly whether this was true. But her silence had already admitted it. Frank had to say something. At the same time, he didn't want to insult Evelyn by renouncing interest.

'Werner, I must say, this is a total surprise to me. I can tell you honestly, this is the first time anything of the sort entered my head.' It was too much of a defence.

'But I am not accusing you, Frank. I will not make you feel like a criminal that has betrayed me. I like you. I want to be your friend. But I think something is going to happen between Evelyn and you and this would make me very sad.'

Frank tries to assure Werner that there is no intentional threat on his side. He cannot speak for Evelyn. Evelyn is still looking at the table in front of her.

'Don't worry, Werner. I have no intention of causing any trouble like that.' Frank wonders what effect this has on Evelyn. Werner continues.

'You see, Evelyn and I, we love each other very much. We never talk about the future but we are very much in love. If this comes to an end, I cannot stop it . . . All the time, I think this will happen. I think it is going to end with us. Evelyn and I have talked about this. She has said you are very attractive. You are very sympathetic. I think this myself. You are a good friend . . . But for Evelyn, I think you are also attractive in a sexual way. I know this is very natural and I cannot stop it. But this will be a tragedy for me.'

Frank's gaze resumes its lap of the table from Werner around to Evelyn in the hope that she will say something. When she remains silent he brings his eyes down to his glass which is now almost empty. The more she continues to be silent, the more he is compelled to dissociate himself from her. But he doesn't want to dissociate himself.

Evelyn has not looked at Frank. Frank cannot look at Evelyn for too long because it would implicate him. Her silence makes him an accomplice. Frank cannot look at his beer for too long because it would confirm a plot. He cannot speak directly to Evelyn because it might be seen as collusion. Anything, even a sideways glance between them, would confirm an ongoing conversation. Frank cannot look at Werner for too long without saying something to deny it. He cannot deny it because he cannot speak for Evelyn. He cannot speak for Evelyn if she hasn't told him what's on her mind. He cannot look at the woman with the urn for too long because it might signify lack of interest. He cannot speak to Evelyn with Werner at the table. He cannot speak to Werner without talking about Evelyn.

Frank must find a way to talk to Evelyn through Werner. Or to Werner through Evelyn. He could talk to his beer with both of them.

'Look, Werner, I will tell you the truth. Evelyn happens to be one of the most beautiful women that I have ever met. I can say that unreservedly. I think you're very lucky. But Evelyn is also a good friend. And so are you. I like Evelyn very much, but that's where it stays. I couldn't possibly imagine anything further happening between us.'

Frank wonders if he is expected to offer to move out of the apartment. But this would also signify admission. He hasn't said enough. But the more he says the more he will admit duplicity. He will soon touch on the ultimate truth that he can imagine anything. Frank is not bereft of desire. He cannot play the eunuch.

Evelyn is playing with a cardboard match which she has torn from the gratis matches; *'Zum Römer, Italianische gerichte'*. Is she trying to tie a knot with the match? She must know that people can see the shape of her breasts through the jumper. Frank's eyes are trespassing. He is caught red-handed. He can only imagine being caught. Imagine being caught coming out of the Eros shop just at that moment when Evelyn is passing by. Imagine being caught in Werner and Evelyn's bedroom. He remembers being caught in an orchard; while he was hiding behind a hedge, the owner was standing right behind him.

Nothing has changed. Except that the restaurant has become more populated now. The more they sit there, the more the real possibilities become extant in their expressions. The more they discuss it the more it becomes true. Frank must take on Evelyn's silence. He must find out whether she is just enjoying a compliment or whether she really has something for him. Frank must speak to Werner on Evelyn's behalf. Perhaps a double negative somewhere might stir the veracity of her silence.

'Listen, Werner,' Frank knows how to look earnest. 'You have absolutely nothing to worry about. You don't have to worry about me and you certainly don't have to worry about Evelyn either. She may have a passing attraction for me, though I haven't noticed. But she really loves you. Anyone can see that. If she was in any way interested in me, we wouldn't be sitting around the table here. It would have been out in the open long ago. She would have said something. I definitely think it's all your imagination, Werner.'

Frank is talking for Evelyn as if she has no mind. He becomes her mouthpiece. Frank can say what she wants to say. He can make her say what she doesn't want to say. He can make her say what Werner wants to hear. He can make her say what he himself wants to hear. He can say what she never intended to say. He can make her say what she wants Werner to hear. He could make her say what she wants to say but doesn't want Werner to hear. He can say what she wants Frank to hear. He can also make her say what she doesn't want to hear herself say. He can provoke her. As long as she says nothing herself, she assents.

'Total fantasy! Any attraction that Evelyn has for me is entirely her love for Irish music. She also likes to speak English. Like everyone else, Evelyn enjoys the company of a foreigner. She loves the music and is fascinated by the way musicians live. In that way, I represent something new. Something carefree maybe. But Evelyn has much more definite views about men. I don't fit into her scheme and never would either. I'm not even her type of man. Evelyn thinks I'm too skinny. I'm too unhealthy. Evelyn would say I'm too much of a man's man. She thinks I'm too much in love with beer and music and good crack. I wouldn't be her sort in a million years.'

The sight of his empty glass between his hands gives Frank the first chance to move outside the circle. He holds his glass up in the air and looks towards the bar. A fishing net hangs over the bar, floating aloft with bottle-green buoys, illuminated with blue-green nautical lights from the midnight Adriatic.

It was almost noon when Evelyn got up. She opened the window and let in the wet, gritty sounds of cement and plastering. It came in repeated sounds of slapping cement. Shovels turning moist cement piles with a sideways slice. A repeated dash of cement against the wall followed by semicircular or circular sounds of levelling. Trowels scooped matter from mortar boards.

Evelyn's breasts rippled like fine plaster. Her hair fell to one side like sand. She turned away from the window and her thighs and bottom shimmered with movement. With one leg already in her trousers, she had to hop on that foot to get into the other side. The skin beneath her white knickers was somewhere between solid state and liquid. Her back bent forward as she stepped into her shoes. It looked matt-varnished. A light-blue jumper hid the remaining skin from the warm daylight. Evelyn first put on her glasses before she turned to speak in a soft, semi-fluid voice. She left behind a cool metallic taste.

Drowning

They were in the pub on Saturday night. In the seat by the partition; the bus seat, they sometimes called it. From there they could see people coming and going through the door. And the line of men sitting at the bar, leaning forward, some looking ahead at the display of spirit bottles, others looking to the right and upwards along the bar at the boxing on TV in the next section. The frenzied sounds of fighting and cheering alternated with moments of toxic silence, a dead hush. Each punch clearly audible.

When her brother came in, Marie decided it was time to have a second drink. She insisted on buying the round, waving her purse in the air, pushing her brother down into a seat with her hands on his shoulders. He smiled and gave in while she went up to the bar and found a gap where she could order. One of the men at the bar glanced at her and nodded before looking down at her shoes. He was leaning forward exposing a gap between his shirt and trousers in which the thin black line of his bottom was beginning to show.

Marie's brother, Joe, was home for the weekend. He talked briefly to her husband John as he took his coat off. Before sitting down again, Joe looked in beyond the partition into the other section, not to see who was there but to get a taste of the atmosphere and perhaps just to see what was on TV. In that section there was a pillar in the middle holding up the ceiling. Attached to it, a golf play-off notice. Elsewhere, it was football posters and a photograph of one of the barmen underneath a WANTED sign.

The two men talked briefly about the drive up from the south. Joe said he had taken the road over the mountains, it was far quicker. Marie acted as the lounge staff, content to be ignored while she placed fresh pints on the small marble table with the wrought-iron legs. For herself she put down another gin, along with a bottle of slimline tonic. It was only when she sat down in the bus seat again that she noticed the exposed bottom at the bar, realizing with some discomfort that it was the man who had smiled and nodded at her. Her husband made a rather vulgar joke about cleavage. It looked like a Wonderbra ad.

Marie looked away. There was always something to be ignored. She talked to her brother about his work.

A young couple came in and sat down close to the door. They sat facing each other, knees touching, occasionally kissing or holding hands. John seemed to be preoccupied with them, staring in their direction as though at a TV. Marie's brother kept talking and after a while, the sight of the couple kissing became too irritating to watch and John joined in with the conversation again. Everybody began to ignore the surroundings. Marie ignored the décolleté bottom and her husband John ignored the intimacies between the couple.

It was as though they had to keep Joe talking, each of them involving him in subjects of their own choice, claiming him for themselves. Marie would bring him back to a family subject, something about relatives in the south. John would grasp the conversation back to politics, showing his cynicism or public outrage at recent events. It was as though Marie and John never spoke to each other, as though they were barred from addressing one another openly.

They spoke to each other only through this third party.

Joe went up and ordered another round, leaving Marie and John behind in silence. What could they talk about? The only thing that came to mind was domestic things. There was the possibility of sex to think about, but not to be spoken about. Marie felt that it was impossible to make love at home because of the children. They could make no noise. It was always silent, as though they had to choke back any emotion or freedom.

But then Marie's brother gave her a signal from the bar, glancing down at the bright, white bottom shifting on the barstool beside him. He came over briefly, bent down and whispered: 'Jurassic Park underwear.' The men stared and mocked at the bottom, but Marie looked away.

Instead she looked at the couple who seemed to have become even more intimate, staring at each other for long stretches before eventually meeting head-on for a long kiss. Each time they kissed, it appeared as though her husband instinctively reached for his drink, as though the two actions were linked by a string. At one point she saw the girl's tongue going in between the boy's lips.

When Joe came back, John asked about the drowning. 'I suppose everybody was talking about it down there,' he said. He had seen all the pictures in the newspapers. 'What I can't understand is how they could put a gravel truck on a thing like that?' Joe confirmed the details of the disaster. In local terms it was another great loss of life which only more vividly recalled the last sea disaster a year before that. Everybody was trying to explain how this latest drowning had happened; there was no logic to tragedy. And suddenly they were drawn into a single, compelling conversation which excluded everything else in the world. The surroundings of the bar seemed to fade into the background. The noise of the boxing died down and was replaced by familiar, transparent ads. Marie and John and her brother Joe concentrated on the drowning; the death of a schoolgirl along with her father was unbearable.

'How can such a thing happen?' asked Marie. Joe began to go through the whole circumstances. It was waiting to happen; the ferry was not seaworthy. The father and his daughter had become trapped when the ferry listed and capsized. It all happened within seconds, yards from the pier, in full view of the locals. One man had dived into the freezing water to attempt a rescue, but failed.

'I feel sorry for the skipper,' Joe said. They talked for a while about the man who owned the ferry, how he had survived, escaping through a window in the wheelhouse. He would surely feel like killing himself. But nobody was blaming him. The locals were blaming the authorities for not subsidizing the ferries; they would stand behind the skipper all the way through the inquest.

They could talk about nothing else but this tragedy. Marie felt at one point that it would be nice to think about something else as well before the night was over. She hardly noticed that John had got up and ordered the last round, only vaguely conscious of the lights flashing to warn of closing time. She had not been aware that the man with the bottom had disappeared, perhaps into the other section, perhaps to the gents' toilet at the back.

When John sat down again, they began to talk about what it would be like to drown. The subject of drowning seemed to have gripped them for the entire evening. They moved away from tragedy to the abstract dynamics of death. The struggle for air, the contamination of the lungs seemed to reinforce the freedom of sitting in a bar and slowly drinking your drink. Marie thought of the father and his daughter underneath the shelter of the ferry, unable to swim up. It filled her with a sense of panic and momentary claustrophobia. They were probably trying to help each other, she thought. She would never try to save herself alone. She thought of the cold water, the feeling of wet clothes, shoes. She was struck by the idea that drowning could be pleasant, if only you could give yourself up to it.

'Once you get a mouthful of water, you're finished anyway,' John said. Even the taste of it in your mouth. You'd feel sick, Joe agreed. Once the water got into your lungs, the panic set in and you had to clear them before you could do anything. He was an expert on sailing. There were plenty of situations where people could save themselves, if they had the presence of mind to know what to do. 'Like Ted Kennedy,' John said, and they were suddenly plunged into a debate on the chances of getting out of a car alive if it went in off the pier. Slowly, the sense of tragedy dissipated. It was replaced by the intense longing for life. Could you break the glass, Marie wondered? Could you possibly open the door? Would you have to keep your mouth shut, wait until the whole car filled up and then try and get out? Joe felt that cars were usually turned upside down and landed in the silt which prevented anyone from opening a door, or even a window. People were often injured or knocked out by the impact. The headlights shining through the water would turn to yellow or luminous green, just like on a very foggy night. There was little chance of coming out alive.

'Besides, it's completely dark down there,' Joe said. He spoke as though he had been down there himself. 'You couldn't see a thing.' The thought of darkness had not occurred to anyone. It consumed them in shock, as though they had had too much to drink and only noticed it when they tried to stand up. They were only half aware of the barman shouting at people to leave. Marie and John seemed to be unable to move, sinking into the absolute darkness of the deep. It would be so silent down there as well, so lonely, so far away from everyone. It would be impossible to think, or call out.

By then everyone had left the pub. The young couple had disappeared too. The TV had been switched off and the barman was beginning to place the stools upside down on top of the bar. He began sweeping the cigarette butts together. Marie knocked back her drink. John found he still had almost a full pint to drink. Marie watched her husband's Adam's apple going up and down as he drank. While she and Joe began to put their coats on, John stood up and raised the pint to his lips, pouring it back in one long swallow, not stopping for breath once, his eyes watering over with the effort before he finally finished and set the glass down again.

Long Before They Knew

It was a strange idea to suggest going back to Corafin after what happened there. Strange coming from him. He watched Olwyn's face for the slightest trace of suspicion or unease as he put it to her. But she reacted with nothing more than a normal, pleased indifference at his choice. After seven years, with two sons aged seven and five, nobody would still attach the same importance to such events. Nobody but him.

Was it conceivable that she had forgotten? Or was it like all the other things they needed to say and discuss so urgently but which never reached the vapour of conversation? Words being too much like accusations. As such, Corafin had always remained the clot of recollection. They never talked about it. You couldn't possibly talk about everything. They couldn't analyse every new development or they would have got nowhere together. Why is she reading the paper? Why have I turned the lights down? You changed your hair. You didn't call me. You've had your breakfast. Why did you say, 'Yes, Robert'? How come you're not wearing the brown shoes? How come you never talk about Royal Terrace? How come he never ever once mentioned Corafin?

Corafin was long before they really knew each other at all. Hardly six months. The driver of the car taking them there pulled in for petrol and got out leaving them to a moment of privacy. The driver had talked incessantly about horses and they had listened or pretended to: the fare of hitchhikers. In that first moment of intimacy during the long drive, he turned to her in the back seat and asked: 'Do you want chocolate?' She nodded and he got out.

And as he picked up the chocolate in the shop, peeling the coins from the counter into his pocket, he noticed through the window that the car was gone. He rushed out, almost ran to the oil-stained, concrete space and saw nothing but the petrol pumps and beyond them, the traffic speeding past on its way to Limerick. He looked every-where and finally saw the car in the corner of his eye around by the side of the building. Annoyed with himself, he walked over and found the driver attending to the tyres, looking up at him through his glasses with a grimace. Olwyn was still in the back seat, surrounded by rucksacks.

He put it out of his mind. The new tension of being attached to someone. He told himself not to care so much. And as they arrived in Corafin late that evening, they walked calmly along the street, the sun throwing long disfigured versions of themselves in front. Olwyn collected the key to her uncle's house while Robert leaned his rucksack against a wall to suspend the weight. On the way up the main street to buy food, a man half sitting on a window ledge nodded to them as if he knew why they had come to Corafin.

A touch of anxiety still remained as Robert picked out the random shopping list. Thinking that she was right behind him in the shop, he was surprised to discover that she was nowhere among the aisles and not to be seen outside either. But once he emerged into the street again he found her sitting on the pavement eating pink biscuits. She offered him one of the teatime wafers but he didn't like them.

They lacked substance. When she asked him to help her get up, he took hold of her hand and just before she could find her balance, he let her down again. She cursed amicably. He did it a second time and caught sight of portions of pink food inside her mouth as she shouted: 'Robert.' So he brought her all the way up, not sure if she was genuinely angry. In fact, nothing was really sure.

The man had disappeared from the window ledge. The street seemed shorter than before. The sun stalled. The mile or so to the large country house seemed more like two or three. Once they were inside the hallway of her uncle's empty house, he pushed her against the wall to kiss her. She tolerated this for a moment, long enough for him to taste the foreign, pink sweetness on her lips before she pushed him away saying she would arrange things upstairs. He offered to make tea and disappeared into the kitchen. A moment later he was back with eggs in his hand shouting up the stairs to ask if she liked eggs, not realizing that she had not yet ascended the stairs and was still there in the hallway, only three feet away. She appeared in the doorway saying, 'It's all right. Nothing wrong with my hearing. There's no need to shout.' Then questioning herself, she answered, 'Yes, I do like eggs,' while Robert smiled and made a half-threat with the eggs.

Later that night, as they walked back from the pub together in darkness, he asked her if she had ever gone horseriding, at which she began to laugh almost uncontrollably into the black fields on either side. He couldn't understand why. There was something else she found hilarious. The smell he described of a neighbour's cat found dead in the attic. How they got talking about breast augmentation or from there on to the subject of roulette and gambling was unclear; but she began to explain or confess or perhaps boast that there was a history of gambling in her family. She described an aunt in Donegal who played routine poker sessions late into the night with the men of the town, adding affectionately: 'She's mad.' Robert was about to ask Olwyn if she ever gambled herself, but instead found himself pushing her towards the ditch saying, 'This way.' She resisted, clutching on to his neck.

Back in the house, they sat for a long time in the kitchen by the light of the back porch on one side and the light from the hallway on the other. They sat on opposite sides of a bare wooden table drinking tea while he watched her eat the last of the teatime wafers. Each small bite was followed by a sup from the mug. Robert was talking about his friend Madden who had gone away to work in Germany. She remembered meeting Madden once but only now became aware of how significant he was. Robert must have missed him. When the biscuits were finished, Olwyn licked her finger and collected the remaining pink crumbs as with a magnetic finger. She sat with her knees bent up listening to the craven things Madden and Robert used to do. She drank the last of the beige liquid before a mud-slide of tea leaves came towards her from the bottom of the mug.

She watched Robert talk. It seemed in the inadequate light that she was not so much looking at his eyes but somewhere past him to the left of his face, at an object on the wall or an imaginary man standing behind him. At one stage, she interrupted him and looked more directly at his eyes. 'You know, you're very strange,' she said. Perhaps more of a compliment. When he asked why, she answered: 'Oh don't worry about it. I just think you're mad.'

It was clear that anything they discussed or revealed about themselves became part of chronological biography. Each had an accumulated image of the other. Because Robert had spoken about going to Germany, she would always link him with a faint thought of leaving for

Germany. It happened before when he talked about his father's raging republican views. Robert would always be the son of a republican. The same went for Olwyn. The image of her became inseparable from Dublin boutiques where she once worked, her older brother's well-known building business, and her father's greyhounds. Though she despised them, there would always be a connection between her and the grotesque sleekness of these creatures which had almost killed her once as a child. She also belonged to the agglomerate impression of singing pubs, launderettes, her friend in the post office, melted cheese on toast and walks around Sutton.

Everything she said joined the inventory. She stopped herself stretching her arms. Robert went over to switch on the radio. After a moment she said: 'That song is trying hard to depress me but I'm not going to let it.'

Olwyn then discovered the sudden urge to tell Robert about all her past boyfriends. She began by saying they never worked out. She never used the word 'men' but instead gave their full names. To Robert, it seemed they were all invented to test him. Derek Hartley was the one person she still had any regard for but he had left her. 'It clobbered me,' she said. His successors were all brief failures, good fun but totally incompatible and bad for her. Like Kevin Armstrong, the musician whose name could often be seen on posters in the city. She had met him on various occasions in pubs and at parties but it wasn't till she ran into him one afternoon in a garden centre that they walked away together holding plants and were in bed together no less than two hours later after drinks in the nearest but most unattractive pub with a pool table. 'Armstrong. He's a right gobshite,' she added as a warning to Robert or to save her own face or in a concealed attempt to say that none of them compared to Robert. She got up and placed her mug on the draining board asking if she should switch off the porch light.

Upstairs, she stood by one of the tall bedroom windows and began to undress functionally with her eyes fixed on distant lights in the town. Robert took time brushing his teeth. When he came back into the bedroom he was surprised to find that she was not in bed but sitting on the low window ledge instead. Having taken all her clothes off, she sat in the window with her knees drawn up to her face, her arms clasped around her knees and her breasts squeezed aside by the pressure against the legs. It made her look colder than she was. More like a child than a woman. Betraying some impatience, he asked her if she intended staying there all night but she didn't reply and merely watched him undress with her head tilted sideways against her knees.

Finally, he went over and with a kiss on each shoulder followed by the lightest kiss on the forehead, as if no other combination would work, as if by palliatives known only to him, he was able to encourage her to yield and move away from the window. In the morning when he woke up, he found himself alone in the bed.

He dressed and went downstairs, but she wasn't in the kitchen. Her book lay open on the table and when he felt the teapot, initially to find out whether it was still hot enough to drink, it told him that she had had her breakfast long ago. He called her, presuming that she was somewhere around the house. He gave up and made tea. It struck him that she might be outside somewhere, so he opened the back door and called out, 'Olwyn. I've made some fresh tea.' In the distance, far beyond earshot, he saw Olwyn making her way back across the fields.

'Is that fresh tea?' she asked, coming in through the open door and finding him pouring from the teapot; as if she had heard his shout across the fields and was now pretending not to have heard it at all.

'I just made it this minute. Would you like a cup?' His offer made it sound like he knew where she was all the time. He got up and plucked a second cup from the dresser. She sat down.

'I'm after walking all over the place,' she said or explained, assuming that he wanted to know where she'd been.

'Really?' was all he said to that. It sounded as though his mind had been utterly engrossed in something else altogether or merely concentrating too much on pouring her tea. His refusal to ask 'Where did you get to?' as would have been expected, brought a hollow resonance.

She reacted, producing a new packet of teatime wafers and placing them in front of her on the table, so much as to say she had been as far as the town. Robert ignored the tacit announcement or failed to notice it and pushed the milk towards her with excessive diplomacy.

'You were fast asleep,' she said almost in answer to a hidden accusation. 'It didn't seem fair to wake you.'

'I didn't hear you getting up at all.' He made it sound like an excuse for not getting up himself, as though he wouldn't have got up even if he had heard her.

She couldn't have been more obvious, drawing further attention to the pink biscuits with the familiar sound of unwrapping the packet. He ignored it again and got up to put on some toast.

'Are you up long then?' he asked with almost naïve interest.

'Ah, I suppose about two hours,' she told him, looking up to see if that answered his question.

There was a pause in which he commented: 'This stove must be ancient,' and bearing the slice of darkened bread over to the table in a grip between thumb and forefinger, he asked the next question as though it had suddenly occurred to him.

'So where did you walk to?' At this stage it made him sound half-witted or childish but she went along with the pretence that he was merely curious.

'I love walking around here. I found this great short cut into town across the fields. The only thing is that when you cross the fields directly, you come across this old abattoir with all these white bones and skulls of cattle lying around.'

Olwyn went on talking for a while until she stood up without warning and said she was going upstairs, went over to his side of the table and took his hand forcing him to abandon his half-empty mug and follow her, which after years of longing for such a moment he didn't know how to resist or slow down to his own pace.

Three days later, Olwyn disappeared completely. The morning had repeated itself. Robert arrived in the kitchen and found her book lying open on the table. He made tea and waited, occasionally looking across the fields in the direction of the town. He wasn't alarmed. He read his book for a while and watched the sun come and go through the kitchen window. Outside he noticed that Olwyn must have done some washing because he saw two pairs of knickers and her jeans hanging in a light breeze on a makeshift line. When she hadn't returned by lunchtime, he went into the upstairs rooms to get a better view over the fields. He gathered she might have stopped at one of the pubs for a drink and got ready to go into town himself.

By the time he had crossed the fields, guessing the short cut Olwyn had found a few days back, it had begun to drizzle. The sky had become dull. Behind him, where he had come from, the house must already have been under the rain. There was little separation between the sky and the pale, grey gauze over the fields.

He reached the abattoir quite by accident, the same way that Olwyn had arrived there. Everywhere, the bleached bones she had spoken of lay around in disarray. In some places they were collected together as if some of the town's inhabitants had made vague attempts to recreate the animals. Elsewhere, the grass and weeds had done their best to bury them. The rain had caught up and begun to spread moisture over the bones, dried by years of sun and wind. Robert could only think back when the abattoir was in use and these cows were stripped of their bodies. Now the weeds grew everywhere around the concrete slaughter-house, reclaiming the earth's old tenancy. A skull, half hidden among the weeds, was obviously missing its eyes and looked more introverted. Time had reversed any degradation and made them more attractive again.

The main street of Corafin looked empty. The people had been driven indoors by the oncoming rain. A car just pulled away from a petrol pump and the attendant retraced his steps. There was a man with a peaked cap standing with his back to the door of a house, sheltering, or trying his best to disappear, like the rest of the town but still knowing something, some unimaginable arena, which kept him on the street. It seemed as though there had been other people in the street until he emerged from the boneyard. A car hissed along the street and stopped, its driver running with hunched shoulders into a house and shutting the door.

Robert was wet when he walked into the pub. Two men standing at the bar turned as though they had expected him and continued talking. Olwyn wasn't there. They seemed to know something. One of them turned to Robert again and said: 'Bad day' as if to avoid any other subject. They were talking about a pump and their conversation centred around whether it could be repaired. Robert ordered stout from the woman behind the bar who began to pull the drink as though she already knew and only waited to hear him say it. She too seemed to be avoiding all other subjects when she spoke about the pump, asking if they would have to go to Galway for spare parts. The idea seemed to amuse the men and one of them said: 'Mission impossible,' at which they all fell silent with contained smiles. Robert took his pint and sat at one of the low tables. One of the men spoke again: 'You might as well put them up again, Bernie.'

He sat in the pub all day waiting for Olwyn. He pretended to read his book. A little girl, two years old or so, ran out from behind the bar and was retrieved forcibly by an older sister. Later, the woman behind the bar who seemed to be facing into two worlds, the household at the back and the public bar to the front, asked Robert a strange question in the plural. She had seen him there with Olwyn before and asked 'Are ye down from the Irish cottages?' to which he answered, surprising himself, 'No, we're staying on the other side of town.' Some hours later he asked her for soup which she granted as a special favour, serving a thin mixture of water and dried ingredients with accompanying slices of white bread. If Olwyn had been there, he would have made an instant joke about it.

But Olwyn never appeared. Later, as more people came into the pub, Robert joined in the pretence and spoke to the two men about the pump and many other local issues. It seemed that everyone was omitting something more important from the conversation. He convinced himself that Olwyn was now back in the house, probably already in bed. The thought crossed his mind too that she might be lying somewhere in a field, motionless, with the rain pouring on her back. But that was uncharacteristic. He reminded himself not to be too apprehensive and rejoined the superficial conversation. It was late by the time he suddenly rent himself away from the talk and hurried back along the road in the rain. There was a light on in the house somewhere, but it turned out to have been left on since the night before. Nothing had changed. Her knickers and jeans still hung on the makeshift line trying hard to collect as much rainwater as they could hold.

Robert stayed at the house for three more days, each day saying to himself that he would leave the next day. Sometimes a gruesome speculation took over which made him want to contact somebody else, or the police even. But he could never imagine Olwyn any other way but in full control of her actions. He searched back through all the things he knew about her to see if there might have been a warning of this somewhere. Through the chronological list. He could only take it that everything about Olwyn had been a warning. Boutiques, biscuits, everything. Her hair. The greyhounds. Sutton.

The next day when he found himself alone in bed again, he decided to leave. He locked the house and left the key back with Mrs Caldwell, deflecting any questions. He started in the direction of Galway and as he walked across the Burren, he felt the tense pleasure of leaving Corafin behind. Out in the Atlantic, he could see the Aran Islands like pieces of animal liver or kidneys floating out from the land. On the Burren, its humped mass of exposed rock, he kept getting the impression that he was walking across a large carcass. In Galway that night, he got a shock when he walked into a pub and somebody waved to him who looked at first like Olwyn. But it was all a mistake.

It was only when he arrived back in Dublin that Robert realized what Olwyn had done. She had gone straight home. Why had he not thought of it? A brief phone call established that she was back in her flat in Sutton again. The number was engaged once but he heard her voice the second time round and put down the receiver as soon as he recognized it. But that seemed to be enough of a signal for her to return the call. Twice he put down the phone when he heard her say, 'Robert', and then 'Robert, it's me, Olwyn.' Then he left the phone off the hook deciding not to talk to her.

The next day she came around to his flat in Dun Laoghaire but he wouldn't answer the door. Somebody downstairs let her in and she got as far as his flat door and began to call him. She came very close, just beyond the door repeating, 'Robert, let me in. It's me, Olwyn.' Even her breathing was audible. His face went white and he felt as though he had been hit by something. He didn't move. He just stood in the middle of the room, motionless, pretending he wasn't there. Until she eventually went away. He watched her through the net curtains walking all the way back down Royal Terrace. The following day, there was a hand-delivered note waiting for him downstairs. It came from Olwyn and said: 'Dear Robert, I'm sorry about what happened. I'm pregnant. Can I come and talk to you?'

Freedom of Speech

The first thing she wanted to do was to travel. Anywhere, everywhere, just to be moving, to see somewhere new. She had recently come out of a bad marriage. It also had to do with a new freedom of movement and the end of the travel restrictions since the Wall came down; because I can, I should. Back in the GDR days, she had never been further away than a Romanian resort. She had once had a bath in a Prague hotel where the water was brown and hot like molten lava. At a nudist colony near Rostock, she got a sunburned bottom and couldn't sit for a week. Travel was not a Soviet concept.

Mostly, it was to the Hartz Mountains that her husband brought her, year after year, forcing her into those heavy walking boots, trudging silently beside him in cement feet, neither of them saying a word. It was all right for him, he was a schoolteacher, but she was an archaeologist and wanted to get to Greece, Turkey, Byzantium, Babylon. In the end she became a desk archaeologist at the Alte Pinothek. The most interesting thing she ever found herself was a porcelain cup which somebody had left on a window sill for a few years.

OK, there had been an expedition to an excavation site on the Polish border which is proven by photographs of her red-freckled face smiling up from dry, dusty trenches, holding up a trowel. In other shots, one of those miniature pickaxes that make you think of Trotsky's head. You don't want to dig too deep on the Polish border, she commented, about the fact that nothing was ever found on the site. The excavation had been purely an exercise. There were shots of her with her husband Gert too, on those Hartz walks with his stick and hat, and a smile of deep-rooted contentment. But of course, he's in the past now, as much as Trotsky or Philoctetes. Or the Berlin Wall.

Mechtild Vogel. She was thirty-two when I met her. Originally from Magdeburg, East Germany, one of the most troubled mid-European towns in history; sieges, fires, hunger and fifty years of dictatorship followed by the abject plunge into the free market. After the bad marriage came a period of feckless promiscuity, naturally. Random uninformed travel which, for an archaeologist at heart, must have appeared like scraping the topsoil for Coke caps. Come on, let's fuck off out of here, she said when we first met.

I found myself standing beside her at one of those human chains against racism, somewhere between Munich and Augsburg. She relit her candle from mine and told me she was getting bored standing around, she had itchy feet. Straight away she announced that it was all over between her and her husband, as though it was the first thing I wanted to know. She was anti-marriage, anti-life partner, anti-house pet, anti anything that promulgated a settled life. 'Up to here,' she warned, raising her finger up level with her long Thuringian nose.

Her apartment was full of artefacts, shards and stones, bits of pottery, all of which came from museum vaults while she worked there. She seemed to have half of the Acropolis in her bedroom and when you went to the loo you found yourself pissing in the company of a stone goat and a Celtic cross. She had no time for Soviet artefacts. There was a champagne cooler which had come from a London hotel. There was a wooden horse with white teeth and glaring eyes and colourful strips of cloth which she had brought back from a *mardi gras*. Her journeys since German unification could only be called casual.

In bed she soon started talking about going places. 'On that fucking thing?' I demanded, pointing at the wide-eyed horse. But she remained serious, as though sex had sparked off a latent nomadic obsession. She understood my concerns and began to explain how she had benefited from the estate of an uncle on the West German side, if that's what I was getting at. Her uncle was a medium-sized advertising magnate to whom she referred as an arsehole, showing nothing but contempt for the money he left her. It tainted her life with the kiss of commerce. But what wasn't tainted these days? Basically we were living in a shagging super-market. So let's get out of here, she urged. Somewhere Third World. She wanted to burn up some of the blood money.

I suggested Morocco and some weeks later we found ourselves in Fez, walking down through the ancient streets, driven into a torpor by the heat. She wore John Lennon-style sunglasses and beat off the flies like a raging pilgrim. She was unable to pass by a fruit stall. In the unremitting Moroccan sun, fruit very soon became the substitute for sex. Any time I looked at her, or half suggested a path towards the bed, she would offer me a tangerine, or a passion fruit, or a banana from Tetuan. In the hotel bedroom, she installed a massive basket, towering with an exotic harvest, grapes hanging over the edges like fat necklaces.

It was as though she had a diploma in fruit eating, meticulously peeling back the skin of a pear with her Swiss Army knife. I watched her with lust in my eyes, juice dripping down from her mouth on to her bare breasts and legs. When I asked her if I could suck the stray liquid from her body she stared back and tilted the fruit basket towards me. My thumb sank into the fruit flesh of a pear, a reservoir of juice spilling across my hands, and I wondered if it was a sign of how ripe the fruit was or how desperate I was.

'I'm still not over my husband,' she explained. She said it with a smile that made me wonder whether the act of smiling had not originated in primal times as a show of aggression and only later evolved into something more dubious. I put it down to the heat. Her suspended sexual interest came as quite a shock. Nothing during the first wild three weeks in her apartment back in Munich could have precipitated this. It was like fucking with a fatwa hanging over you. We hardly stopped to eat. All right, she ate melon slices while we were screwing, but I never imagined fruit taking over.

I looked for an explanation. She had seen some fairly distasteful things along the journey around Morocco; faeces, backing-up toilets, that kind of thing. We saw flies drinking from the corners of children's eyes. Once I gave a small girl in Ouarzazate a tin of sardines and she ran home with it like a prize. In the night we heard a woman in an alley below our hotel window being beaten by her husband, or brother, or pimp. The sound of a fist meeting a face has an unmistakable smack of reality about it. A woman offered me her seven-year-old daughter for the afternoon. In a mountain village Mechtild watched, in a demented way, a boy crossing the road carrying a cow's stomach like a sack over his shoulder and leaving a trail of purple spots along the road. It was more 'Third World' than her wildest imagination.

Would this put you off sex? I argued with her. Threatened to go home if she wasn't interested. The human body had a duty towards pleasure and happiness. The heat made us talk in circles. Thirst made us belligerent. Above all else I wanted to sort out this discrepancy between fruit and sex. Her lack of lust seemed to have degenerated into a purely linguistic problem rather than a physical one. Could sex not be an exchange of fruit fluids? It was a problem of definition.

In the late hours at our Fez hotel, with the bedroom window open on to the din of the old city, the sickle moon stuck on a blue-black sky, we decided to clarify every word. Even if we had to invent a whole new vocabulary for our relationship, it was essential that we redefined the exact meaning of each word as it pertained to us.

Fruit: the closest thing to fucking. Fez: medieval Moroccan city visited by many Americans and Germans in shorts and sunglasses. Thirst: a physical (sometimes metaphysical) imbalance which increases at every attempted reduction.

Outside our hotel the following morning, we met Mustafa. He became our guide, simply because he announced that he was our guide. I first tried to shrug him off but Mechtild quite liked the idea of being shown a few things. So we spent the day following Mustafa through the hyperactive souk with its dealers and donkeys and symphonies of smells. Every street had a thousand eyes. The eyes of women in *haiks*. The eyes of traders. The eyes of bald, lethargic dogs, motionless in the shade. The eyes of chickens bound together at the feet, five in a bunch. And the eyes of Moroccan men, each of them skilled at telling exactly what is going on inside your head.

Travel: extended foreplay. Tourist: a person coming from the last orgasm and on the way to the next.

Mustafa knew what was on Mechtild's mind. He pulled her aside to sit under an awning where he brought her some orange juice. Her thirst was getting out of hand. Three times she had to stop for juice. Mustafa showed us everything;

where to eat, where to find the best pastries, where to drink lemon tea and watch the swallows over the city walls while the evening shrank back into a blue, yellow, then black night. Somewhere close by there was always music, drums and whistles. Mechtild was happy. She became generous. She searched in her bag and gave Mustafa some money, more than he ever expected. Then she put her head on my shoulder and watched the moon over Bab Boujaloud.

Money: that which makes the bearer attractive beyond all order of merit.

Back in the hotel bedroom I asked her why she had given Mustafa so much money. Was it some new substitute for sex, this generosity to strangers? Still there was nothing doing between us. I had completely lost my powers of persuasion. My penis stood up in the room, massive and inappropriate, as out of place as a missile marked for nuclear disarmament. I told her Mustafa would expect the same money the next day. It was her money, she said. She had too much of it. She would never get rid of her past until she got rid of the money.

The following morning I went out early after breakfast while Mechtild stayed at the hotel. She was exhausted: when I came back before lunchtime, I met Mustafa on his way down the stairs. He was running. He told me he had been sent out for my lady. Cream crackers.

Mechtild, my lady, was just about to take a shower when I got to the room. I lay on the bed listening to her body under the water. Music from the radio somewhere drifted in around my ears like the high-pitched whine of a mosquito. I could hear the water cascading down, accelerating over the slope of her breasts, across her hips, leaping on to her raised knee. I imagined drinking the cool water as it rolled off her bottom. I must have fallen into a dream of paralysed lust. After a while the water stopped and by the time Mustafa came back, she was dressed again, wearing a long, loose white T-shirt with a pink elephant on the front.

Breast: that which fits perfectly into a cupped hand. Cream cracker: dry, square-shaped biscuit of unstable, flaky composition. Lust: modern-day slavery.

I got up and stepped into the bathroom to shave. In the mirror I could see Mustafa standing at the door with the packet of cream crackers in his hand. Mechtild asked him to come in and sit at a small table. She placed the cream crackers in front of him. From her money belt she took out a crisp new 100 DM note.

'Do you know how much this is worth?' she asked.

'Yes,' Mustafa nodded.

'Well,' Mechtild went on. 'If you eat this whole packet of cream crackers, the money is yours.'

Jesus, I couldn't believe it. Mustafa took it up as a perfectly normal challenge and sat down. He looked at the cream crackers, checked Mechtild once more to make sure she wasn't joking, and then began to eat while Mechtild lay back on the bed fanning herself with the pristine blue banknote. The shape of her nipples showed through the T-shirt.

'What the fuck are you doing?' I whispered, the lather on the left side of my face giving me a speech impediment.

'Don't interfere,' she said.

Encouraged by the sight of the 100 mark note which Mechtild was now rolling into a fine tube, Mustafa voraciously threw himself into the meal of cream crackers. There was nothing with the cream crackers, no cheese, no drink or anything. He didn't get very far before his mouth began to clog up. His chewing slowed down. He attempted to swallow. His head moved forward and back with the effort. His mouth was open, full of pulpy white dough. The heat didn't help.

'Give him a glass of water at least,' I urged.

'That's not part of the deal,' she insisted.

I told her she was carrying it too far and she conceded, giving Mustafa a capful of mineral water. If anything, the water only made matters worse. It was like masticating patching plaster, or fireclay, and very soon his chewing came to a complete standstill. He looked pale. He made another brave effort to swallow and then allowed his head to sink down in defeat. A large, white ball of dough rolled out of his mouth across the table and fell to the floor.

'I'm sorry,' Mechtild said. 'You did very well, though.'

Mustafa sat there dejected. To encourage him, she told him he might have another chance the following day. Same time. He was to bring a new packet of cream crackers.

'You can't do that kind of thing,' I said after Mustafa had gone.

'Why not?' she laughed, putting away the unfurled banknote. 'Why the hell can't I? It's only a bloody game.'

'You can't fuck around like this down here. You can't behave like a complete arsehole in the Third World.'

'Don't start,' she sneered.

I watched Mechtild reach for the blue plastic bottle of Sidi Harazam mineral water. The water ran down her neck inside and outside. The radio was still playing outside somewhere in the distance. It was too hot to talk.

The following day, Mustafa came back to try the game again. A new packet of cream crackers was placed on the table. Once again he was eager to get on with the meal. This time Mechtild added a new incentive. Along with the 100 mark note, Mustafa could also have her. For my benefit she loudly said, 'You eat the whole packet, you have the money and you can also fuck me.' She pulled up the T-shirt to let

Mustafa see her jet-black triangle. Pointing towards him with her finger, she then patted her cunt lightly with the tips of her fingers. For a moment I thought she was going to place the 100 DM note in there.

The money was one thing, but the additional promise of sex made Mustafa dizzy with ambition. He ate like he was starving, swallowing the first few cream crackers whole. Again around halfway, the feast slowed down. His mouth lugubriously churned the floury paste like a cement mixer until it got stuck altogether. With tears of failure in his eyes he extracted a long baton of grey dough from his mouth and dropped his head.

Game: the act of contriving superiority along abstract rules. Cunt: that for which, and in which, a man would suffocate of his own volition.

Later on that evening, we met Mustafa again in a bar. He was as friendly as ever. He seemed undisturbed by failure, accepted the fact that he had given it two good chances. I bought him a few beers in consolation. He was eager to try the cream crackers again the next day, but Mechtild said she wasn't offering another chance. He swore he could do it. He got drunk very quickly and proclaimed that we were his greatest friends. He loved Europeans deeply. He wanted us to meet his family, his brothers and sisters, his mother.

'You come to my house,' he said suddenly with a glazed expression.

'No, not now,' I said. 'It's too late.'

'No, no. Tomorrow,' he begged. 'You come to my house. You and your wife. My mother will cook for you – very good. You must come and eat the couscous.'

The idea of Mechtild being my wife was a delicious piece of irony. She ignored it.

'Of course we'll go,' Mechtild said, jumping at the idea. I think she was doing it only to dislodge the grin on my face.

'At last,' she said to me later, back at the hotel. 'A chance to see what family life is like in these countries.'

Next day, Mustafa was waiting for us outside the hotel door. Everybody seemed to have forgotten all about the cream cracker game. I had forgotten what sex was like. We followed him through the narrow streets of the Medina, through a maze of alleys all leading downwards. I lost all sense of direction. I knew only that we were descending into the heart of another ancient civilization, Mustafa occasionally pointing out things with great excitement: his school, the tanneries, the mosques. We followed him through the narrow alleys, gazing around in awe. He showed us doors or houses which had two knockers, one for horsemen, the other for pedestrians. All the time he was saying, 'Not far, not far,' and finally brought us into a quiet alley, no wider than a metre, where we had to walk in single file.

'Here is our house,' he eventually announced.

Mechtild was beside herself with excitement. Her eyes were wide open. We stepped inside and were led into a small room at the back. As soon as I entered the room I got the feeling I wanted to reverse everything, go back to zero, like a board game. We were surrounded by four men. They couldn't all have been Mustafa's brothers.

Mustafa whipped the sunglasses off Mechtild and put them on himself before she could react. We were told to sit down on the floor. Mechtild smiled as though it was all a joke. She defied them at first but then she realized that things had gone wrong. Mustafa's manner changed completely. He took her bag. Our possessions were piled on the stone floor in front of us: passports, money, traveller's cheques, American Express cards. Cameras, watches, guidebooks, and Mechtild's contraceptives. Why the fuck she had those with her I don't know. The last things that came out of her bag were two beautifully ripe pears. One of Mustafa's brothers bit into one of them, smiling. I could hear the smack of the fruit chunk giving way, his mouth sucking up the exploding juice with it. It was as though he had just taken a bite out of Mechtild's breast, as though I was forced to watch him screwing her. I wanted to kill him. I might have if it were not for the fact that Mustafa now held Mechtild's Swiss Army knife in his hand.

'What are you doing?' Mechtild shouted indignantly. Maybe she was still pretending not to understand.

'You find out now,' Mustafa said, picking up some of the traveller's cheques to examine them. He had already pocketed the blue 100 mark note which Mechtild had shown him the previous day. I had visions of Mechtild eating hundreds of cream crackers. Maybe it was heat, maybe it was fear. I imagined Mechtild and Mustafa coupling on a bed of cream crackers.

Fear: narrowing of the anal passage. Shitting cream crackers.

I felt the Swiss Army knife at my throat. In the corner of my eye, I could see that Mechtild had a long rusty blade at her throat too. The hair at the back of her head was in the grip of a fist. There was a faint smell of urine in the room. There was no sound anywhere.

'All right,' Mustafa said out loud. 'This is a very simple game. We are not going to take all your money, just some of it. You will go to the bank and get cash. One first, then the other one.' I saw Mechtild giving me an incredulous look. Maybe it was fear. Or maybe she had begun to regret the missed opportunities, all those wonderful orgasms I could have arranged for her. Maybe she was thinking of my poor penis standing like a folly on the landscape.

'You get the money,' Mustafa said. 'Then there is no

trouble. I will go with you. OK. Who wants to go first?'

So this is what sex leads to. If it wasn't for lust we wouldn't have been in this mess together. I told Mechtild to go first, hoping that she would have the sense to make a break for it as soon as she got to the bank. I encouraged her with a discreet wink. She got up and allowed herself to be escorted to the door, from where she looked back giving me a silent, desperate glance, perhaps thinking of all the fruit we could still have eaten together in our lifetime. Mustafa dropped his knife on the floor and, as he bent down to pick it up, I saw him lick the calf of her bare leg. Mechtild jumped as though she had been licked by a rabid animal. Then they were gone.

I wasn't expecting her back. When she returned half an hour later, I was worried. She looked pale and exhausted. She was soaked in sweat. Her brown legs were shining in the heat.

'Allah will be pleased,' Mustafa said as he pocketed the money.

It was my turn to go to the bank. I tried not to look at Mechtild but Mustafa stopped me and made me look back. I couldn't make out if she was in tears or whether it was beads of sweat in her eyes. She said nothing. Nor did I. The point of a knife slightly altered the perfect roundness of one breast beneath her damp T-shirt.

Penis: instrument of war and pleasure. Allah: a man with a penis so big it strikes terror into the heart of all nations. God: a man who falsifies the size of his own penis. Believer in the afterlife: a man who can fuck himself.

On the way to the bank I must have thought of a hundred ways to get out of the trap. Mustafa would not talk to me. We passed a group of American tourists and for a moment I thought I could ask them to help. There was nothing I could do. I had to remain loyal to Mechtild. My last memory of her became unreliable in the heat.

At the bank, I stepped towards the counter to get the money as required. The money didn't matter. A small price for Mechtild's freedom. I had visions of us back at the hotel again, free, penniless, making love like maniacs, fucking again like people in a war zone. Maybe all this would teach her a lesson. Fucking is all that matters in this world. But then I had a stronger urge to fight my way out. I turned suddenly and threw my arms around Mustafa, clutching on to him like a drowning man, trying to drag him down with me, shouting all the time, 'Thief, thief.' But nobody seemed to pay any attention. It was like a stupid embrace. I must have appeared like somebody who had lost his reason in the intense heat, a tourist with sunstroke, malaria, bilharzia. Mustafa punched me discreetly in the stomach as he struggled free. He made it look like he was helping me to lie on the floor, to rest myself. Within seconds, he had disappeared into the crowded street outside, leaving me in the doorway bent over, with the eyes of onlookers penetrating my skull.

Loyalty: a self-imposed virtue characterized by the eagerness to sink with others in preference to surviving alone. Sex: sinking together. Oral sex: singing without accompaniment. Erection: the power of illusion. Love: the science of self-deception. Corpse: a body no longer capable of giving or receiving pleasure.

I ran to the police, but there was little point. There was no way I could give descriptions or lead them to the house where Mechtild was being held. And all the hours running around the Medina looking for her proved just as futile. I got lost every time. All I had now was my money and my passport.

Three days later, Mechtild turned up at the gates of the old city: Bab Boujaloud. I found her sitting in a small café staring in front of her at a lukewarm glass of mint tea. I rushed over to her. I was so excited to see her alive. Was she unharmed? I couldn't see.

She would not let me embrace her or comfort her in any way.

'Mechtild, are you all right?' I said emptily under her passive stare. 'Those bastards. I tried everything to find you. I was so worried about you. The police were out everywhere. I did everything I could.'

I might as well have spoken to a corpse. She stared straight ahead, her eyes vitreous with hurt and indifference.

'What happened?' I asked.

'I'm going home,' she said without looking up.

Nothing I could say would change her mood. I asked her how she got the bruised lip. I wanted to know had they done anything to her? Had they raped her? Had they taken all her money? I took her away and got her something to eat. All she would accept was soup which she spooned slowly past her swollen lip. She was starving.

'What happened?' I asked again. 'What did they do?'

When she said nothing, I began to explain and invent reasons for why I had acted to save myself. Mechtild wasn't interested. She held up the spoon to stop me talking. The flies kept bothering her and I tried to chase them away. It was useless. She looked past me, staring at the traffic in the street outside, at the laden donkeys, at the people waiting for buses in the distance.

Spoon: instrument for conveying soup.

Fly: thoughtless insect.